Heartland

~

True Enough

by Lauren Brooke

SCHOLASTIC INC.
New York Toronto London Auckland Sydney
Mexico City New Delhi Hong Kong Buenos Aires

QUIZ # 76521
ARBL 4.6
Points 5.0

With special thanks to Gill Harvey

For Gidon Saks — a good friend with a big heart

If you purchased this book without a cover, you should be aware that this book is stolen property. It was reported as "unsold and destroyed" to the publisher, and neither the author nor the publisher has received any payment for this "stripped book."

No part of this publication may be reproduced in whole or in part, or stored in a retrieval system, or transmitted in any form or by any means, electronic, mechanical, photocopying, recording, or otherwise, without written permission of the publisher. For information regarding permission, write to Scholastic Inc., Attention: Permissions Department, 557 Broadway, New York, NY 10012.

ISBN 0-439-33967-7

Heartland series created by Working Partners Ltd., London.

Copyright © 2003 by Working Partners Ltd.
Published by Scholastic Inc. All rights reserved.

SCHOLASTIC and associated logos are trademarks and/or registered trademarks of Scholastic Inc. HEARTLAND is a trademark and/or registered trademark of Working Partners Ltd.

12 11 10 9 8 7 6 5 4 3 2 1   3 4 5 6 7 8/0
Printed in the U.S.A.   40
First printing, March 2003

Chapter One

"Come on, Boxer," Amy encouraged, stroking the bay cob's neck gently. "Just a few mouthfuls."

She offered Boxer a handful of alfalfa cubes. He blew at them, then turned away, his eyes dull and uninterested. Amy sighed. He hadn't eaten a single one, and he had barely touched his hay net. In fact, he had refused to eat for the last three days, ever since arriving at Heartland.

"What's wrong, Boxer?" Amy asked softly. She scratched his forehead, studying his large, noble face. "I wish you could tell us."

Boxer's head drooped, and he turned away from Amy to face the back of his stall. She'd have to leave him for now and try something else later. She was letting herself out of the stall when she saw Ty, her boyfriend and one of Heartland's two stable hands, coming down the barn aisle.

"Here, I brought you something," said Ty, handing Amy an apple and a carrot. "If he won't eat these, he won't eat anything."

Amy smiled. "Thanks. It's worth a try."

Amy approached the cob again, half an apple in her outstretched hand. To her relief, Boxer took it and chewed slowly. "Good boy!" said Amy. "Now here's the other half."

But Boxer ignored her and stood still, a dribble of apple foam hanging from his soft lips. Amy offered him the carrot instead, but Boxer turned away again.

"It's no good," said Amy. "He's not interested. I think he needs more time to settle in and get used to things around here."

"Maybe," agreed Ty doubtfully. "But it's been three days."

Amy nodded, frowning. Horses varied so much. Some adjusted to a new home immediately, while others found it harder acclimating. But three days was a long time for any horse to be off his food completely — unless there was something wrong.

❧

Amy let herself out of Boxer's stall, and she and Ty headed out of the barn. Amy went to saddle up her own horse, Storm. The jumper thrust his gray head over his stall door and whinnied eagerly as she approached, his eyes shining. Amy smiled. The contrast between Storm and Boxer couldn't be more striking — Storm was alert and eager, full of energy and life. Amy needed to help him channel that energy for the show they were entering on Saturday.

"Let's see what you're made of today," Amy told him as she tightened the girth. "I'm going to raise the jumps another three inches. What do you think about that?"

Storm snorted and flicked an ear at the sound of her voice. Amy grinned. She led him out into the paddock and mounted.

In the training ring, Amy warmed him up. He was fresh and danced playfully, but Amy rode him through his paces, working on his rhythm and balance. Soon he had calmed down, his neck a graceful arch as he accepted the bit. Amy took him over some low fences, to prepare him for jumping the course. He hopped over them easily with an energetic flick of his tail, and Amy knew he was ready. She dismounted and tied him up while she quickly raised the fences.

In the saddle again, she felt Storm quiver with excitement as she turned him toward the first jump. There was a surge of power as the gray horse took off beneath her. She could tell, even as his hooves left the ground, that they would clear the fence with ease. As Storm landed,

Amy looked through his alert, pricked ears to the jump ahead.

"Easy does it, Storm," she murmured, collecting him. He sized up the parallel bars in front of him, and Amy eased her grip on the reins. In two long, powerful strides, Storm reached the jump and soared over it, his front hooves tucked neatly under him. With just as much ease and grace, Storm cleared the straw bales and a simple spread fence.

"Only three more to go," whispered Amy, turning Storm toward the combination. It was a double. As he cleared the first jump with inches to spare, Storm was already eyeing the second. Amy barely had to ask him to shorten his stride before he was over, and she was guiding him toward the last fence. Storm snorted as he approached it and gave a confident toss of his head. He cleared the vertical, and Amy's face broke into a grin. They had ridden clear.

"That was amazing!" she praised him, clapping her hand affectionately on his neck. As she slowed him to a trot, she heard the sound of more clapping, this time from the edge of the ring. She looked over and saw Ben Stillman, the other Heartland stable hand.

"Hey, Amy!" Ben called. "He's looking good!"

Amy smiled and rode Storm over to where Ben's tall figure stood by the gate.

"He is, isn't he?" she agreed. "He's just flying. I can't wait till Saturday."

"I hope Red will be in top shape by then, too," said Ben.

Amy slid down from Storm's back, and Ben opened the training ring gate for her. She led the gray gelding out, and they walked up to the stable together.

She and Ben were both competing on their horses a lot this summer. Ben had been showing for years and had great plans for himself and his chestnut gelding, Red. But for Amy, things were different. When she wasn't at school, most of her time was taken up with the Heartland horses — finding solutions for their problems and healing them of the pain they'd suffered in the past. Until this summer, she'd competed on her pony, Sundance, but she'd never taken it very seriously.

Now she had Storm. The thoroughbred was a gift from her father for her and her sister, Lou. Amy was working at all hours so she could find time to compete on him regularly.

"I'm so relieved vacation has started," said Amy as she and Ben reached the stable yard. "I can give Storm a really long rubdown without feeling like I should be somewhere else."

Ben grinned. "Well, he sure deserves it after that performance," he said.

Storm nudged Amy with his nose and snorted. "And doesn't he know it," Amy said with a smile, mussing Storm's mane playfully.

❧

By the time Amy had finished with Storm, there were long shadows across the stable yard and the last of the evening sun was casting an orange glow on the white farmhouse. Amy headed indoors, suddenly feeling very hungry. She washed her hands and sat down at the supper table, where the others were talking among themselves.

"How's Storm going, Amy?" asked Jack Bartlett as he helped himself to some potatoes.

"He's like a dream, Grandpa," Amy said enthusiastically. "I raised the fences this afternoon, and he flew over them. His strides and his timing are just perfect."

"I was watching," agreed Ben. "He and Amy are looking fantastic. They've got a good chance of winning Junior Jumpers on Saturday."

Amy flushed at Ben's words of praise. She looked over at Ty, who smiled at her warmly. It was typical of Ty to be supportive, even though he wasn't into the show scene at all. They had started dating about six months ago, but he was her best friend long before he was her boyfriend.

"It's a good thing vacation's finally here," said Lou, frowning slightly. "You've been looking exhausted lately, Amy."

"It's been a lot for you to manage," agreed Jack Bartlett. "School, the regular Heartland work, *and* competing."

"You know, I've been thinking ahead," said Lou. "We need to figure out what's going to happen when you go back to school. It's just too much work dealing with Storm on your own."

"But there are still weeks to go!" protested Amy. "And besides, I *was* doing fine before."

"Like I said, you were looking exhausted," insisted Lou.

Amy gave her older sister a troubled look. Lou was right. When it came to being practical and taking a rational view of things, she usually was. "So what do you suggest?" Amy asked, not sure she'd want to hear the answer.

Lou seemed slightly embarrassed and lowered her eyes for a moment to spear a carrot on her fork. Then she looked at Amy honestly and said, "Well, actually, I was wondering if I should help more with the horses."

Amy put down her knife and fork in astonishment. Lou didn't like to spend much time working with the horses. But before Amy could give a response, Lou continued. "I don't know how else we're going to manage.

It's obvious that you won't be able to keep up your workload when you're back at school, Amy. It's just too much. And we can't afford another stable hand. So it seems like the only sensible option."

Upon hearing Lou's generous offer, Amy instantly felt guilty. Her sister had enough on her plate already. If it weren't for her, Heartland's business would be a shambles. Since their mother, Marion, had died the previous summer, Lou had more or less saved Heartland from closing with her sound financial sense and ideas for making money. But her fear of horses had meant that she'd never really been involved with looking after them.

There was something else, too. Their father, Tim, lived in Australia, and until a few months ago hadn't seen his daughters for thirteen years. He had been shocked to discover that Lou had stopped riding. After his visit, Lou decided she would try riding again, but it would take some time to overcome her fear. Although Storm had been a gift to both of them, there was no way that Lou could ride him yet, and Amy couldn't help but feel bad about it. Now it looked like Storm was creating more work for Lou, too. Amy smiled at her sister awkwardly.

"It's great of you to offer, Lou," she said. "But really, we can cope. Honestly."

Lou sighed. "Well, I guess we'll have to see how it goes," she said. "When you're back at school, we'll have a better idea of whether you're keeping up with everything. But I have to admit that I'm worried. We have a waiting list at the moment."

"We've had a waiting list for ages," said Amy. "Isn't that a good sign?"

"Yes and no," said Lou. "If people have to wait too long to get their horses into Heartland, they begin to wonder why we haven't cured the horses we have."

Jack Bartlett looked thoughtful. "That's a good point," he said. "Are any horses ready to go? How's Boxer?"

Amy shot Ty an anxious glance. Boxer had come to Heartland because his owner couldn't take care of him anymore, not because he had a particular problem — or so they'd thought.

"No, not yet," said Amy. "He's having problems settling in, and he's not eating. We can't really find him a new home until we're sure he's OK. And anyway, we need to find out what he's like and what kind of owner would suit him."

"Well, maybe that's something to keep in mind next time we get a call like that," said Lou, slightly impatiently. "We're not a dealer's yard. And we have enough —"

"I know, I know," interrupted Amy.

Amy knew what Lou wanted to say. What with Sundance, Red, and now Storm, there were enough horses at Heartland that didn't need treatment. Perhaps if Lou had taken the call from Boxer's owner, rather than Amy, the horse wouldn't have been accepted. One of Heart-land's most important principles was that every horse should be rehomed or returned to its owner as soon as possible, to make room for other horses that needed help.

To her relief, it was Ty who spoke next. "There may be more to it with Boxer," he said. "We were thinking that he was just having trouble settling in, but it really shouldn't take this long."

"He arrived on Sunday, didn't he?" asked Grandpa. "That was three days ago. Well, he should be OK by now."

"Yes," agreed Ty. "And it's not only that he's not eat-ing. He's dragging. There's no life in his eyes."

"Perhaps there's something that Ruth didn't tell you, Amy," said Grandpa.

Amy thought about it. Ruth Adams, Boxer's owner, had been evasive on the phone. She had said that her work was piling up on her and that she just didn't have the time to give to Boxer. She'd heard that Heartland was a good place for unwanted horses. Amy had started to ask why Ruth couldn't just sell him herself, but Ruth had cut her off. "He's just too much," she'd said. The edge to her voice had made Amy give in.

She nodded, frowning. "Maybe there *is* something else," she agreed.

"Has Scott checked him over?" asked Lou. Scott was the local equine vet and Lou's boyfriend.

"Not yet," said Amy.

"Well, the sooner he gives Boxer a clean bill of health, the sooner we can find him a new home," said Lou.

"I know," said Amy. Lou was right, of course. But the vision of Boxer's dejected form swam in front of her eyes, and she had a feeling that things weren't going to be quite that simple.

✧

When supper was over, Amy and Ty headed out to the yard to do a final check around the stalls. It was a warm summer night, with stars twinkling overhead. The yard was quiet, apart from the gentle sounds of horses pulling at their hay nets.

Amy left Ty to check the front yard while she went to prepare a wormwood infusion for Boxer, which she hoped would increase his appetite. Then she headed for the back barn. All the horses were quiet. Some gave gentle snorts of greeting when they realized she was there. She let herself into Boxer's stall and placed the bucket in front of him.

As she stood watching him anxiously, she leaned over the half door, and Ty joined her. He put his arm gently around her shoulder, and she leaned into him as they studied the horse. Boxer was nosing the bucket. He took one mouthful but then lost interest.

"Not working, huh?" said Ty in a low voice.

Amy shook her head. Wasn't there something that could tempt him to eat? A gust of warm summer air blew down the barn from the open door, and she had a thought. "He's probably used to being turned out more, especially in summer," she said.

"Well," Ty said, "it's more natural for him to graze than to eat from a hay net."

"Let's turn him out tomorrow," said Amy. "We can see if it makes any difference."

"And I'll call Scott first thing in the morning," said Ty. "Just to make sure there isn't anything really wrong."

Quietly, they turned away from the stall. Ty kept his arm around Amy, giving her shoulder a slight squeeze of reassurance. Despite all the difficult times they had come through over the last year, she and Ty had gradually drawn closer. It was good to feel they understood each other so well, especially when it came to treating the horses.

But as they reached the end of the barn, Amy looked back at Boxer. She hated seeing a horse look so unhappy.

Ty shook his head. "Don't worry," he said softly, as though he could read her thoughts. "We'll figure this out."

Amy gave a little smile. So many horses had found an answer at Heartland, but there was always the chance that one wouldn't. "I hope you're right," she said with a sigh. "I really hope you're right."

Chapter Two

"Easy does it, Red," murmured Ben, leading his chestnut toward the ramp of the trailer. "Come on, boy."

Storm whinnied a greeting to his companion from inside the box, and Red clattered up the ramp to join him. It was Saturday morning. With Storm and Red loaded up, Ben and Amy were ready to go.

"You're off?" asked Ty, appearing from the feed room. Amy nodded.

"Well, I'll try to get over to watch your class, if I get through everything here," said Ty. "Standbridge can't be more than a twenty-minute drive."

Amy was touched. Ty hardly ever came to shows, so she knew he was only coming for her sake. "I'd like that," she said gently.

Amy climbed up into the trailer next to Ben, who

started the engine. Ty raised his hand. "See you later," he called as they pulled out of the driveway.

✎

The show ground was already bustling with life when Ben maneuvered the trailer into position. Amy rushed out and ran to undo the bolts. Inside, Storm was already bright-eyed and eager, sensing the atmosphere around him. He was a born competitor and loved the thrill of show days.

"Come on, down you go," said Amy, backing him out. She tied him up outside the trailer, then went to the registration tent to pick up Ben's and her numbers.

"Your first round is coming up," she told Ben when she got back. She handed him his number. Ben had already tacked up Red and was ready to start his schooling session.

"I thought it would be," he said. "Thanks, Amy. I need to get moving. I'll see you in a while."

He rode off, and Amy turned her attention to Storm. "Let's get you warmed up," she said to the gray gelding, who was swishing his tail and stamping his hoof impatiently. "I know you want to get going."

She tacked him up and trotted down to the practice ring. At the sight of the jumps, Storm's ears pricked forward, and he danced on the spot in excitement. But something else had caught Amy's eye — Ashley Grant.

Ashley was in Amy's class at school. She was beautiful and wealthy and scoffed at Amy's work at Heartland. Her mother, Val Grant, ran a stable called Green Briar, which churned out neat, polished ponies using methods very different from those of Heartland. Ashley had always done well at shows and had recently moved up a level, so Val had bought her a talented Danish warmblood called Bright Magic. They would be competing in Junior Jumpers alongside Amy and Storm, and Amy knew they'd present a real challenge.

Ashley was taking Bright Magic over the practice jumps. Her impeccable golden hair was perfectly held in a hair net beneath her velvet riding hat, and her clothes were, as usual, immaculate. She and the high-spirited chestnut made a striking pair. But to Amy's surprise, it was clear that, just at this moment, their performance was far from spectacular.

The fences were high, much higher than Amy thought wise for a practice session. With Storm, Amy wanted to loosen his muscles and build his confidence, not stretch him too much. But Ashley clearly had a different approach. Or perhaps it was her mother's idea, because Val was shouting instructions from the side of the ring as Ashley took Bright Magic over the fences.

As Amy rode closer, she brought Storm to a halt and stared. From here, she could see that Ashley's horse was wearing a harsh Kimblewick bit, and he was also pulled tight in a restrictive standing martingale. She watched as Ashley turned toward the first jump in a combination. The chestnut plunged forward. Ashley, usually so poised, had difficulty controlling his approach as he lunged at the jump and hurled himself over. With Val shouting more instructions in a furious voice, Ashley brought her crop down on Bright Magic's flank, then managed to collect him and aim toward the next jump. The horse snatched at the bit and rushed toward the fence, then took another huge leap and cleared it with a foot to spare.

Amy raised an eyebrow. "Well, he can jump," she said softly to Storm, patting his neck. "But he's not looking too happy about it."

She turned her horse down the side of the practice ring and began trotting him in circles and figure eights. Storm was soon balanced and on the bit and ready to ride over some fences. Amy took him to the far end of the ring, where some lower fences were in place. Storm had just cleared them comfortably when Amy heard a familiar voice.

"Afraid to try him over anything bigger, Amy?" Ashley called, riding past on Bright Magic. "I always knew you'd shy away from making the big time. You don't have the taste for success."

It was no surprise when Ashley let loose with insults. Amy had experienced it enough times. She stared after

Ashley's disappearing back and stroked Storm's neck, then she shrugged.

"Let's ignore her, all right?" she said to Storm, who flicked back one ear. "She's not worth it."

❧

Back at the trailer, Amy tied up Storm and hurried over to the main ring where Ben was riding in the Intermediate class. He'd done really well over the last few weeks and had even won Intermediate Champion at a recent show, so he was hoping to continue at that performance level, if he could.

Amy found a good position at the side of the ring just as Ben rode into it. The bell rang and he was off. Amy watched as they approached the first jump. Red was looking impressive.

"Go for it, Ben!" called Amy, willing him on. The jumps at this level were daunting, but Amy knew that they could manage them. Ben had a determined look on his face, and as they steadily cleared fence after fence, Amy's excitement rose.

Red tucked his feet up over the final jump, and Amy broke into applause. They'd done it again! She hurried around to the ring entrance to meet Ben, and they headed back to the trailer together.

"Wasn't he good?" said Ben. "I hope Storm goes as well for you."

"Yeah, well, it's my turn soon," said Amy. "My class has already started. I'll be on in about twenty minutes."

To Amy's delight, Storm's performance was every bit as strong as Red's. Calm and responsive, he eyed the jumps fearlessly and sailed around clear. It was looking like a good day for Heartland.

"We've got a while to wait until our next rounds," said Ben. "I'll get us a couple of burgers."

"Great," said Amy. "I'm going to watch the rest of my section."

When Ben rejoined her at the side of the ring, the next rider was Ashley on Bright Magic. The chestnut was looking no more settled than he had in the practice ring; if anything, he looked more worked up. Flecks of foam covered his neck, and he snatched at the bit, his eyes rolling every time he caught sight of Ashley's crop, which she gripped tightly in her right hand. The bell sounded, and Ashley turned him toward the first fence. Bright Magic pranced on the spot as Ashley fought to maintain control. Then, as she released her grip on the reins, he surged forward, making an unbalanced leap over the fence. As they landed, Ashley looked frustrated. She tapped the crop on his flank and hauled him into line again as they approached the next jump. The same pattern repeated itself: Bright Magic rushed forward, then overjumped, looking more precarious and worked up at every fence.

Amy watched with her heart in her mouth. All her sympathies were with Bright Magic — she hated to see any horse make such hard work of jumping, no matter who owned him. She thought of Storm's pricked ears and fluid movement. Right now there was a world of difference between the two horses.

"They'll be lucky to make it around," said Amy to Ben in a low voice.

"Something's wrong," Ben said. "He looks way too uncomfortable."

But with only two jumps to go, Ashley and Bright Magic were still clear. The second-to-last jump, the wall, was positioned right in front of Ben and Amy, near the edge of the ring. It was fairly straightforward but had to be judged carefully because there was no spread of poles to help gauge its height.

Amy heard the chestnut's labored breathing as he approached. Ashley, flushed and frowning, was sawing at the reins to keep him in check until two or three strides before the jump. She eased her grip, and Bright Magic began his usual desperate approach. Then, suddenly, one stride before takeoff, he skidded to a halt, his hind legs sliding under him.

Ashley, fully expecting a mammoth leap through the air, was already well forward in her saddle. She flew over the horse's head and into the wall with a sickening crunch. The crowd gasped.

Acting purely on instinct, Amy ducked her head under the ringside rope and grabbed hold of Bright Magic's reins.

"Ashley!" she called as the stewards ran anxiously toward the wall. "Are you OK?"

Ashley staggered to her feet. She looked deathly pale, but at least she was in one piece. As the stewards quickly reconstructed the wall, she staggered back toward her horse. Amy was prepared for Ashley to quickly snatch the reins away from her and remount without so much as a thank-you. But as she reached forward to take the reins from Amy, her hand trembled and she averted her eyes.

Amy stepped back and ducked under the rope again. The crowd watched Ashley uncertainly. Would she finish the course, after a fall like that? She stood still and leaned her forehead against Bright Magic's neck. The seconds passed. It was clear that she wasn't going to mount again. One of the stewards approached her and gently took the horse's reins from her hands. Ashley didn't resist. Another steward took Ashley's arm, and horse and rider were led from the ring. The crowd applauded sympathetically.

"She's in shock," Amy whispered to Ben. "I'm not sure she knows what happened."

"Yeah, that looked bad," said Ben.

"The horse had had enough," said Amy. "You really can't blame him."

"I guess not," agreed Ben. "He had no sense of control out there."

"You know," said Amy, "I know it's Ashley, but I feel like I should go and see if she's all right."

"That is so like you, Amy," said Ben. "I guess I'll come, too."

〰

They threaded their way through the crowd to the ring entrance. There, slightly to one side, stood Bright Magic, Ashley, and her mother, Val Grant. Val was clearly furious.

"Have you any idea how much I paid for this horse?" she was shouting. "The least you could have done was *complete* the course."

Amy and Ben stopped in their tracks. Ashley stood, head bowed, as her mother grabbed Bright Magic's reins.

"And now," bellowed Val, "you're going to get back on and take him over the practice jumps. There's no excuse for cowardice. I'm not having you think you can get away with a performance like that."

Ashley raised her face. If anything, she looked even paler than she'd looked just after falling off. She didn't speak but gave a desperate, pleading shake of the head. Val stepped toward her, brandishing Bright Magic's reins.

"*Get — back — on — this — horse!*" she demanded through gritted teeth, her eyes blazing.

Amy had never seen Ashley look so crushed. She stood with one hand over her eyes, her shoulders shaking. "I — I *can't*," Amy heard her say in a trembling voice.

Amy felt a surge of anger at Val's bullying tactics. Ashley was obviously too shaken to ride properly. She looked dazed. She should probably be lying down somewhere.

"*Can't* is not a word we use," snapped Val. Then, impatiently, she swung up onto the chestnut's back herself and rode off toward the practice ring. Ashley was left on her own, staring after her mother's disappearing back.

"She's a monster," muttered Ben.

Amy nodded her head in agreement.

They watched as Ashley started to follow her mother. But she seemed shaky on her legs and weaved slightly as she walked.

"Something's wrong with her!" exclaimed Amy, starting forward. "Ben, we'd better take her to the first-aid tent."

They hurried after Ashley, and Amy grabbed her arm.

"I'm — fine," said Ashley faintly as her knees began to buckle.

"I don't think you are," said Amy firmly.

Ben took her other arm, and between them they walked Ashley to the medical tent on the other side of the ring. A nurse greeted them, and Amy quickly explained what had happened. Soon Ashley was lying down.

"My — my mother," Ashley stuttered.

"Don't worry," said Amy. "We'll let her know you're here."

The nurse smiled at Ashley. "Looks like it could be concussion," she told her. "We'll need to get you checked out. You might just be shaken up. Either way, it's nothing that rest won't cure."

Ashley nodded and sank her head back on a pillow.

"We'll go and find your mom, Ashley," said Amy.

Ashley's eyes met Amy's for an instant, then slid away. She looked miserable but angry, too.

"Thanks," she said grudgingly.

🐍

Ben and Amy headed for the practice ring. They saw Val riding Bright Magic out of the area at a brisk trot. Amy hailed her. The woman's face still looked like thunder.

"Ashley's in the first-aid tent," Amy informed her coldly.

Val scowled. "First-aid tent? What on earth is she doing there?" she asked. Then, without waiting for an answer, she rode on.

"What is wrong with that woman?" exclaimed Amy, staring after her. She watched as Val rode over toward the Green Briar trailers. One of the stable hands ran to meet her — someone Amy recognized. It was Daniel.

Amy had gotten to know Daniel recently. She had met him and his talented mare, Amber, at a show. He'd been doing well on the circuit when disaster had struck and Amber had to be put down because of an injury. Then, to make things worse, he'd lost his job. So when a job had come up at Green Briar, he'd taken it. It had looked like his only hope for a future working with horses.

Val dismounted and flung Bright Magic's reins at Daniel, then marched off in the direction of the medical tent. Amy saw Daniel beginning to soothe the lathered horse as he led him away.

"Look, Ben, I'm just going to say hi to Daniel," Amy said.

Ben frowned, checking his watch. "We don't really have time," he said. "The first round of Junior Jumpers has just ended. I heard the announcement on the loud-speaker."

"But I haven't talked to him since he started at Green Briar," said Amy. She felt bad thinking about it. She gazed after Daniel, who was now heading out of sight behind the Green Briar trailers. She felt torn, but Ben was right. She'd have to talk to Daniel some other time. They hurried back to Storm and Red.

"Good luck," said Ben when Amy had mounted again. "I don't know if I'll be able to watch — our times are very close together."

"Thanks," said Amy. "I'll come right over to your ring when I've finished."

Pushing Ashley from her mind, Amy took Storm down to the practice ring and settled him onto the bit again. He was in good form, keyed up for the competition but responsive to Amy's requests. She then headed Storm to the ring to see how the second round was progressing. There were only two more riders before her, so she walked Storm around the gate area to keep him warm. Suddenly, she spotted a familiar figure walking across the show ground. "Ty!" she called, urging Storm into a trot.

Ty grinned and came toward her.

"Hey! How's it going?" he asked.

"We went clear in the first," Amy told him. "And so did Ben. I'll be on in about ten minutes."

Ty stroked Storm's neck. "Good boy," he said. "You keep him warm. I'll go and get a good place in the stands."

Amy looked at him. "I'm glad you're here, Ty," she said, smiling.

There were only seven fences in the second round, but they had all been raised by a few inches. When Amy entered the ring, she was feeling confident. She pushed Storm into a fast canter and turned him toward the first fence, a parallel spread. As Storm pricked his ears and sailed over, Amy grinned to herself. This was going to be good. She kept up the momentum and pushed Storm as fast as she dared, but she didn't want to unbalance him. More than anything, she wanted to ride clear.

When they cleared the final fence and heard the ripple of applause, Amy knew they'd done well.

"That was number 431, Amy Fleming on Summer Storm," announced the loudspeaker. "Clear, with a time of eighty seconds."

Amy felt her heart sing. With a time like that, she was pretty much guaranteed a place, even if she didn't win the blue ribbon. She trotted from the ring and found Ty waiting for her at the exit.

"Nice job," he said with a smile.

"It's not me, it's Storm." Amy laughed. "He loves it." She slid down from Storm's back. "I think that was the fastest time yet," she added, running up the stirrups. "But there are still plenty of riders to go. I'll be really happy if we place. Let's head over to the other ring to watch Ben."

They were just in time to catch Ben's round. The fences in the Intermediate competition were now truly daunting, and only a few horses had been clear so far.

He and Red attacked the course with enthusiasm — too much enthusiasm, perhaps. They thundered around at an astonishing speed, and the crowd held its breath. But at the second-to-last fence, Red's speed caused him to flatten a little as he jumped, and he clipped a pole with his hind feet. Four faults. But Ben rode from the ring looking only slightly disappointed.

"Well, we can't win them all," he said to Ty and Amy afterward as they walked back to the Junior Jumpers ring. "It's always good to reach the jump-off, and we haven't been riding at this level for long. At least you still have a chance of taking home a ribbon!"

They discovered that only one rider had a faster time than Amy — and there were only two more to go in the class. They watched the first anxiously, a guy of about Amy's age on a piebald. They had a disastrous round and collected eleven points — two poles down and a refusal.

"I don't know how they went clear in the first round," commented Ben. "They probably don't do as well at faster times. Now you're at least third, Amy."

She nodded, feeling an anxious knot in her stomach. They watched the final pair, a determined-looking girl on a sleek Trakener cross.

"They look like they mean business," muttered Ben. "Dangerous."

He was right. The horse was jumping well, and the

girl shaved off time by turning him tightly whenever possible. They looked certain to go clear, and sure enough, they didn't so much as tap a fence.

"That was number 576, Jessica Bailey on Mahogany," announced the loudspeaker as applause rippled around the ring. "Clear, in a time of eighty-five seconds."

"Amy! You did it!" whooped Ben. "That puts you in second!"

Amy was delighted. As she rode back into the ring to collect her ribbon, she waved to Ty and Ben. Ben waved back enthusiastically, while Ty smiled at his side. Amy could tell he was trying very hard to feel as excited as she and Ben felt. She just had to accept that however long she competed, it would never be Ty's thing.

"You go with Ty, Amy," insisted Ben, back at the trailer. "I don't mind driving the horses home."

"Thanks, Ben. We'll catch you later."

She and Ty made their way off the grounds, with Ben following in the trailer. Once on the road, they sped up and soon lost the slower vehicle.

"Scott came to see Boxer this morning," Ty told Amy. "He says there's nothing wrong with him, at least not physically."

"Well, we're going to have to find out what's up, then,"

mused Amy. "We still can't let him go to someone else —
not until we're sure he's OK."

"No," agreed Ty. "Anyway, no one would want a horse
that looks so dejected."

Amy sighed and looked out the window. Ruth Adams's
attitude about Boxer was puzzling. Amy knew all too well
how time-consuming some horses were, and that could be
very difficult for owners with a lot of other responsibili-
ties. But Ruth hadn't even brought Boxer to Heartland
personally. She'd arranged for a neighbor to transport the
horse in his trailer. It was as though she couldn't wait to
get rid of him.

The thought of any horse being bundled off like that
was painful to Amy. Poor Boxer. Amy resolved to spend
more time with him over the next couple of days. So
much more was possible during the vacation — she
could give more individual attention to all the horses,
more time to Storm, and, she thought, smiling to herself,
she got to see Ty more, too.

Just then, she noticed that they were passing the
turnoff to Ty's home. Amy had a sudden idea.

"Ty," she said impulsively, "we could go and visit your
mom and dad. I'd love to meet them."

Ty looked at her quickly, an astonished expression on
his face.

"Meet my *parents*?"

"Well, why not?"

From Ty's expression, Amy could see he wasn't so sure. He smiled awkwardly and glanced at his watch. "I don't think we have time right now," he said. "We need to get back to do the evening feeds."

"We wouldn't need to stay long," said Amy. She looked at Ty closely, but he said nothing. "Do they know about me, Ty?" she asked softly.

Ty shifted in his seat. "Sure they do," he said briefly, keeping his eyes on the road. Then he turned and gave an uneasy smile. "Look, I just don't like springing surprises on them, OK? Maybe some other time?"

"Sure," said Amy. "That's fine."

They lapsed into a slightly uncomfortable silence. Amy felt upset. Why didn't Ty want his parents to meet her? Was he ashamed of her? She'd always assumed he was proud of everything about her. If there had ever been any doubts about their relationship, they'd been hers, not Ty's.

She tried to think of another way to approach the question, but she couldn't think of one. Talking more about it would just have to wait for another time. But somehow she had a feeling that Ty wouldn't be the one to bring it up.

Chapter Three

"I'll ride Dancer again," said Lou, carrying her saddle out of the tack room. "I think she's good for my confidence."

"Fine," said Amy. "I'll take Major. He's almost stopped bucking now, and a trail ride will do him good."

It was the following afternoon, a beautiful summer Sunday, and Lou had decided to join Amy on a trail ride. She had only started riding again a few weeks before. As Amy watched her sister tack up and mount, she thought how much more confident Lou was beginning to look. They headed onto the driveway and past the paddocks, where many of the Heartland horses had been turned out to graze. Amy shielded her eyes from the sun, surveying the scene. In the left-hand paddock, Storm grazed peacefully next to Sugarfoot, a tiny Shetland pony.

Since his arrival, Storm had picked out Sugarfoot as his special friend, despite their difference in size. Then there were Red, Jasmine, and Spring all together, cropping a lush patch of grass.

But one of the horses was apart from the others, at the far end of the paddock. It was Boxer. The cob was standing on his own, his head hanging low. Amy drew Major to a halt, and, as they watched, he shifted his weight listlessly from one hind foot to the other but otherwise didn't move.

"He's not even grazing," said Lou.

"No," said Amy. "And he's been here a whole week now."

"But didn't Scott say there's nothing wrong with him?" said Lou.

Amy nodded and nudged Major forward again. "There must be some reason why he can't adjust," she said, sighing. "I'll give Ruth Adams a call."

When Lou and Amy returned from their ride, Amy headed indoors and looked up Ruth's phone number. She punched it into the phone and waited.

"Hello, Meadowbridge," said a voice.

"Hi, Ruth?" said Amy. "It's Amy Fleming at Heartland. May I ask you a few questions about Boxer?"

"Why? There's no problem, is there?" asked Ruth.

"We're not sure," replied Amy. "I was wondering if you could tell us a bit about his history. He hasn't settled in well and isn't eating."

"Is that all?" said Ruth, sounding relieved. "Well, I'm sure there's nothing wrong with him. He was fine when he left here."

"But it's unusual for a horse to take so long to adjust," persisted Amy. "There must be some reason."

"Oh, he's probably just missing Hank a bit," Ruth said dismissively. "That's my father. Boxer belonged to him."

Amy was surprised. This was the first she had heard about Ruth's father. She cast around for the right question. She had a feeling that Ruth was trying to put her off. "Does your father know that Boxer is here at Heartland?" she asked.

"Of course he does, yes, yes," Ruth responded, a little too quickly. "But he hasn't ridden for a while. It was time for Boxer to go. Now, I'm very sorry, but I was just about to go out when you phoned."

"But," asked Amy desperately, "did they spend a lot of time together?"

"Who? Hank and Boxer?" Ruth gave a nervous laugh. "Why, like any other horse and owner, I guess. Now I've really got to go."

"But —" began Amy, then she realized that the phone had gone dead. Ruth had already hung up.

Amy stared at the phone, frowning. Why hadn't Ruth told them about her father? *He's just too much*. That's all she'd said about Boxer before. But in what way? Was it Boxer's behavior that was *too much*? It wasn't adding up. Ruth was hiding something, Amy was sure, but why? She headed out to the yard and found Ty mixing the evening feeds.

"I thought I'd make a start on these before bringing the horses in," he said. He looked up from the feed bins and saw her face. "Hey, what's wrong?"

"I've just been on the phone with Ruth Adams," said Amy. "Boxer wasn't her horse after all. He belonged to her father, Hank."

"And her father wasn't the one who sent him here?"

"No," said Amy. "A bit strange, don't you think?"

"Maybe," said Ty. He scooped some alfalfa cubes out of a bin, his brow furrowed. "I've been thinking about Boxer's behavior," he said. "I've only seen horses behave like that when they're pining, when they're missing someone. Think of Sugarfoot and Pegasus."

Amy nodded. The same thought had begun to occur to her. When Sugarfoot's owner had died, the little Shetland had almost pined away. Only when Lou started singing to him, as his owner had done, had the Shetland taken an interest in life again. And Pegasus — dear, dear Pegasus. After the accident that had ended her father's career, Amy's mom had nursed him back to health at Heartland. Then when her mom died, Pegasus also withdrew. It was the grief, combined with cancer, that had killed him. A lump rose in Amy's throat as she thought of the wonderful horse she had grown up with and how she missed him.

"But," she pointed out, pushing the thought aside, "Hank isn't dead. Ruth just mentioned him and said he knew Boxer was here. Why would he let Ruth get rid of his horse if they're so attached to each other?"

"I don't know. It doesn't make any sense," Ty agreed.

"And Ruth's not being very helpful," said Amy. "I think we need to talk to Hank."

🖎

When Ty had finished mixing the feeds, he and Amy headed down to the paddocks to bring in the horses.

"Lou and I rode past Boxer earlier," Amy told Ty. "He was just standing on his own. Not grazing or anything."

As they approached the paddock, they could see that nothing had changed. He had barely moved.

"Poor boy," sighed Amy, opening the gate. "I'll try T-touch in his stall. It might comfort him a bit."

She went to get him and led him to the barn while Ty brought in Storm and Sugarfoot. In Boxer's stall, she began to work along his back with her fingers, making tiny rhythmic circles up toward his withers and neck. As she did so, she felt his muscles relax, and he dropped into a doze. Amy didn't stop. She continued working up his neck, murmuring softly to him.

A shadow fell across the stall door, and Amy looked up. She nearly fainted when she saw who it was.

"Ashley!" she exclaimed. She was the last person on earth Amy would expect to visit Heartland. "What do *you* want?"

"Thanks for the welcome," said Ashley. She flicked her hair back over her shoulder and smiled.

Amy stopped working and stared at her coldly. Given the way that Ashley always spoke about Heartland, she was hardly *welcome* here. What did she expect? And here she was in the back barn, snooping around.

"How did you find me?" Amy asked. "Did someone tell you I was here?"

"Finding you wasn't that difficult, Amy," Ashley said sweetly. "After all, there are only two stable blocks to look around."

Amy glared at her but decided to ignore the comment. She let herself out of Boxer's stall.

"So aren't you going to ask if I'm OK?" asked Ashley.

Amy remembered Ashley's fall. She was clearly none the worse for it. "Well, I can see you've recovered."

"Yes," said Ashley. "I should be riding again in a couple of days."

Amy started to walk out of the barn. Whatever Ashley had come for, Amy wanted to get rid of her as quickly as possible. Heartland was none of her business.

Ashley followed her. "So how did you do in the end yesterday? On Storm?" she asked.

Amy stopped in her tracks and turned to face the other girl. "Look, cut the small talk, Ashley. What do you want?"

Ashley looked startled for a minute, then she smiled. She cleared her throat and hesitated. "I was wondering if you have my crop," she said eventually. "I left it somewhere yesterday. It belonged to my grandmother. Did you pick it up?"

"No," said Amy, shrugging. *Is that all you want?* she thought. She paused and thought back over the previous day's events. "I don't remember seeing one at all, apart from when you were riding. Sorry."

Ashley fiddled with one of her perfectly manicured fingernails. "My mother will kill me," she muttered.

"What?" asked Amy.

"Oh — nothing," said Ashley quickly.

Amy opened the barn door, and they headed up to the stable yard.

"What were you doing there with that cob?" Ashley asked in a gentle voice. "What's wrong with him?"

Amy looked at her quickly. Ashley's face was all innocence, but Amy didn't trust her. Why would she want to know about Boxer or any of the horses at Heartland, for that matter? Maybe she *was* snooping. Maybe her mother had sent her. She wouldn't put it past her. "Ashley, you didn't come here to ask about your riding crop, did you?" she asked bluntly.

Ashley blanched slightly. "Yes, I did," she faltered. "I told you. It belonged to my grandmother. It means a lot to me."

"But if I had picked it up, I'd have called and told you," said Amy.

"How could I know that?" asked Ashley sulkily, her composure quickly restored. "For all I know, you'd keep it."

Amy felt a rush of anger, but she also felt slightly reassured. When Ashley was being her usual self, at least she knew where she stood.

"That's not true, and you know it," Amy retorted. "So what *are* you doing here?"

Ashley hesitated, her proud features creasing into a frown. She flicked back her golden hair again. She seemed on the point of saying something, then changed her mind. Ashley smiled her perfect smile again and made for the driveway. "Well, sorry to have troubled you," she said as she walked off. "Bye, Amy."

Amy glared after her retreating back. "She's too much," she muttered to herself and turned away.

"Hey, Amy! Wasn't that Ashley?" asked Ben's voice, coming up behind her a moment later.

Amy nodded. "Yes. It was."

"Why was she here?" asked Ben curiously. "Is she OK after yesterday?"

Amy gave a wry smile. "She's fine," she said. "Well enough to come snooping, anyway. I don't know why else she would have come. She had a silly excuse, but I don't believe it."

Ben shrugged his shoulders innocently. "Maybe she meant to thank you for yesterday," he said, "but couldn't bring herself to do it."

"Yeah, right," said Amy, picking up some stray straw from the stable yard. "And then she'd ask me to go for ice cream."

❧

Amy quickly dismissed Ashley's mysterious visit. Ty had brought in the rest of the horses and had more or less finished distributing the evening feeds. In the summer months, this was a quicker job than in the winter because the ponies only needed a hay net to supplement their grazing.

"I'll start doing the water, Ty," she called across the yard as he emerged from the feed room. She worked around the front yard, carrying buckets from the stalls and refilling them with fresh water from the yard tap. When she reached the back barn, she wondered if Boxer was feeling any better. His stall was quiet as she approached, and she glanced over his half door.

"Boxer?" she called, unable to see the cob at first. She moved closer and peered over his door. He was lying down, his head hanging low, his muzzle almost touching his bedding. Amy hurriedly let herself into his stall. To her relief, Boxer scrambled to his feet but then simply stood watching her, his eyes dull.

Amy sighed and stroked his nose. "Boxer," she murmured, "you sure are one unhappy horse." She picked up his water bucket and let herself out of his stall again. "We need to talk to your *real* owner," she told him.

Amy headed into the farmhouse and found the Adams's number. She dialed the number. It was Ruth who answered.

"Hi, Ruth," said Amy. "It's Amy Fleming again, at Heartland."

"Amy," said Ruth warily. "What is it this time?"

"Well, Boxer still hasn't adjusted," said Amy. "I was wondering if I could speak to your father."

"My father?" exclaimed Ruth, sounding alarmed.

"Yes. Is he there? I mean, does he live with you?" asked Amy.

"Why do you need to speak to him?" demanded Ruth, ignoring Amy's question.

"We think that Boxer may be missing someone," explained Amy. "It's the most likely reason for his behavior. And if your father was his owner, he's the most obvious person."

There was a brief silence on the other end of the phone. "You can't speak to him," said Ruth eventually. "He's not . . . available at the moment."

Amy felt as though she was trying to squeeze water from a stone. Ruth just wasn't giving her anything. "I understand. But perhaps you could talk to him?" she persisted patiently. "Perhaps if we could see them together, if he could visit, it would help us establish whether this is the problem or not."

There was another pause. "Well, I guess we could try to arrange a visit. If you really think it's necessary," Ruth replied wearily. Amy got the sense that she just didn't want to accept that Boxer had a problem.

"Thank you," said Amy, trying to ignore Ruth's reluctance. "It would help us enormously. When do you think he could come?"

"I'll figure it out with him," said Ruth briefly.

Amy thanked her and replaced the receiver. *How odd,* she thought. Ruth was so unhelpful and clearly thought Amy was a nuisance. And she made her father sound so mysterious. What was going on?

Chapter Four

Amy was still staring at the phone when it rang. She picked it up.

"Amy?"

"Matt!" exclaimed Amy, astonished to hear the voice of her old friend.

"It's been a while, hasn't it," began Matt, sounding slightly nervous. His voice trailed off.

"Well, I guess so, but you're always welcome to call — you know that," Amy said slowly. "Anyway, I'm glad to hear from you. How's it going? What's new?"

"Oh, this and that," said Matt evasively. "There have been a few . . . changes recently, that's all. I wanted to see if you'd like to go for coffee. Maybe next week."

"Sure," said Amy. "That would be good."

She was itching to ask him what he meant by "changes" but resisted the urge. He would tell her in his own good time.

"How's Thursday?" asked Matt. "At Jerry's, say ten-thirty?"

"Sounds good to me," said Amy. "See you then."

Later that evening, Amy added some black pepper to the chicken and mushroom sauce she was making. "Allow to simmer," she muttered to herself as she looked at a cookbook. Then she filled a pan with water, put it on the stove, and added some salt. "Salt to taste."

Lou was out with Scott, and Grandpa was visiting friends, so Amy had offered to cook Ty dinner. Cooking wasn't her strong point, but it wasn't often that she and Ty got to spend an evening alone together.

"It smells good," Ty said, coming in from the yard. "What are you making?"

"Don't get too excited," said Amy, grinning. "It's just a chicken and mushroom sauce. To have with pasta."

"Sounds good to me. Better than my mom's cooking these days," said Ty, sitting down at the table and taking off his boots. "Do you need a hand?"

"I'm almost done, thanks," said Amy. "What's the matter with your mom's cooking?"

Ty frowned. "Oh," he said, "she just doesn't cook much these days."

"So your dad does it all?" Amy was surprised.

Ty looked uncomfortable but laughed it off. "I don't think my dad's ever seen the inside of a kitchen," he said. "And my mom's idea of cooking is opening a box of frozen food and putting it into the microwave — at least that's how it's been for the last few years."

Amy shook some pasta shells into the pan of boiling water. *Ty knows all about my family and what we've been through,* she reflected. *But I hardly know a thing about his — and maybe he doesn't want me to.* The thought made her feel uncomfortable. She knew that his family didn't understand his love of horses or his work at Heartland — especially not his dad, who was a long-distance truck driver. Amy was also aware that his mom had health problems, but they'd never talked about it. She stirred the pasta and checked the sauce, then sat down at the table.

"Your mom's not well, is she?" she asked tentatively, realizing how awkward she sounded.

Ty played with the silverware that Amy had laid out on the table. "She's depressed, if that's what you mean," said Ty.

Amy hesitated. "We don't have to talk about it. Not if . . ."

"You know I want to share my life with you, Amy,"

said Ty. "It's just that there are some things that I prefer not to think about very often. Not while I'm here."

Amy nodded. "Sure," she said softly. "I understand."

Standing up again to check the pasta, she turned down the heat. "Almost ready," she said.

Ty grinned. "Great," he said. "I'm starving."

❧

As they ate, Amy told Ty about her conversation with Ruth Adams.

"She didn't sound too excited about Hank visiting, but she eventually agreed to it," she told him. "I think there's something she's not telling us. Either that, or she's a very strange woman. She's kind of thorny."

Ty speared a pasta shell with his fork. "It is odd," he agreed, "that she didn't let you speak with Hank personally. Did she say why?"

"No, she just said he wasn't available," said Amy.

They thought about this in silence as Amy served seconds.

"You know, I could pick Hank up on Tuesday," said Ty. "I'm taking the morning off to help my mom out. She's asked me to do some shopping for her. I could stop by Ruth's place on my way here. The address is somewhere near Davidstown, isn't it?"

"Yeah," said Amy. "That's a good idea. If Ruth agrees to it."

"Let's call and ask after supper," suggested Ty. "So we can get it over with."

Amy nodded. At that moment, she was only half thinking about Ruth. It had suddenly struck her how much Ty did for his mother.

"Can't your mom do the shopping herself?" she asked.

Ty looked embarrassed.

"Sorry," said Amy hurriedly, "I didn't mean it that way. It's just —"

"It's OK," said Ty. He sighed. "She's having a rough time right now," he explained. "When she's like this, she can't leave the house. It's too hard for her. And Dad's off on a long job, so it's up to me to do the shopping. It's fine. I don't mind."

Amy stared. "How long has she been like this?" she asked, feeling unsure what to ask next.

"Well, she's fought depression since I was about ten. She isn't always down. It kind of goes in cycles."

"When she gets down, how long does it last?"

"It depends. Weeks. Sometimes months."

"And what about your brother?" Amy was very vague about him. She knew he was younger than Ty, but that was about it.

"Lee?" Ty shrugged dismissively. "He just sits around watching baseball. Or keeping his Playstation company."

Amy didn't know what to say. Ty finished his pasta

and reached for Amy's plate. "That was great," he said. "I'll do the dishes."

"Leave them," protested Amy. "I'll do them later." She stood up. "Let's call Ruth."

🐍

Amy was surprised and somewhat relieved when it wasn't Ruth who answered the phone, but a man. An old man.

"Hello," said Amy. "Is that Mr. Adams?"

"Why, yes," said the man. "Mr. Adams. That's right. Who are you?"

"This is Amy Fleming, at Heartland."

"Ah, yes, yes," said Hank again.

"I'm calling about Boxer," explained Amy. "He's your horse, isn't he?"

"Boxer's my horse, yes," said the old man, sounding delighted. "He's my special boy."

"Well, I don't know if Ruth has mentioned this to you," said Amy, "but we're wondering if you could visit him, here at Heartland."

"Of course," replied the old man. "I would like to see my boy. When would you be coming?"

Amy hesitated for a moment. "Someone could pick you up on Tuesday, if that's convenient."

"Tuesday. Tuesday. That's good," said the old man.

Amy felt relieved. "I'm so glad you can come. We've been worried about him. He hasn't been eating."

But Hank didn't respond. He'd already put the phone down.

❧

Amy stared at the receiver, then over at Ty.

"That was Hank?" asked Ty, raising an eyebrow.

"Yes," said Amy, putting the phone back in place. "He said he would come and see Boxer on Tuesday. You can pick him up."

"Great!" said Ty. "Well, there's obviously no great mystery, then."

"No," said Amy uncertainly. "Though he was a little strange on the phone. And he put it down before I'd even had a chance to finish. Ruth did that, too. They're an odd pair."

Ty shrugged. "Well, it takes all sorts," he said. "We'll just have to see how it goes on Tuesday. I'll get out the map."

❧

Amy got up at six the following morning. She pulled on her jeans and a shirt and headed out to the yard. Ben and Ty didn't arrive until seven, so she had an hour to herself. She grabbed a broom and swept the yard. Then she decided to clean out the trailer. After tidying up in the back, she climbed into the cab to give it a once-over.

She opened the door on the passenger side — and stared. There, on the seat, lay a riding crop. She picked it up. It was made of old, well-polished leather and had what looked like an ivory handle. Amy examined it more closely. There were letters engraved on the handle. Ashley Jane Weaver, she read. Could this be Ashley's crop? But how?

Amy heard the sound of a pickup coming up the driveway and quickly climbed out of the cab. It was Ty's, but Ben's was following about a hundred yards behind. She said a quick good morning to Ty, then waved to Ben as he parked.

"Ben!" she called, waving the crop.

"Hi, Amy," he said, getting out of the pickup. "What . . ." He stared at the crop and instantly clapped his hand to his forehead. "Amy! I completely forgot. I must have taken that out of Ashley's hand when we helped her to the medical tent. I kind of held onto it without thinking, then threw it into the cab when we got back to the trailer."

"And I went home with Ty, so I didn't see it. I can't believe it's Ashley's — and it's here," said Amy. "Ashley Weaver must have been Val's mother."

"I wonder why she didn't mention it when she came yesterday?" asked Ben.

"She did," said Amy. "But I thought it was just an excuse. I said I didn't believe that was the reason she came by."

"Hey, I'm sorry," said Ben, laughing. "It's my fault for not telling you."

Amy grinned. "I'm sure Ashley will have managed without it for a couple of days," she said. "Besides, she's not riding at the moment." She twirled the crop in her fingers, then pursed her lips, thinking of Ashley's behavior the day before. "But do you want to know something?" she added.

"What?" asked Ben.

Amy tapped her boots with the crop and shook her head. "I still don't think it's why she came."

Amy phoned Green Briar later that morning. It was Daniel who answered the phone.

"Daniel!" exclaimed Amy. "How are you? I saw you at the show, but I didn't have time to come over."

"Hi, Amy. I saw you, too," said Daniel. "I watched your first round." He dropped his voice. "But after Ashley's fall, there was no way I could come and find you. Val Grant had everyone running around like crazy."

"I can imagine," said Amy. "But are things OK otherwise?"

"Fine," said Daniel. "It's a bit weird here, but I'm working with horses. That's the main thing." He paused, then said, "Listen, Amy, I've got to go. I've got three horses to groom before the next lesson. It's really nice to talk to you."

"I understand," said Amy hurriedly. "Look, I was just calling to say that we've found Ashley's crop, here at Heartland. Can you tell her for me?"

"Sure," said Daniel. "See you soon."

Amy finished the morning chores and checked on her pony, Sundance, who was still recovering from a tendon injury. The swelling was almost gone, but it still wasn't possible to ride him or let him out into the paddock. After rewrapping his bandage, Amy headed inside for lunch. As she ate a sandwich at the kitchen table, she realized that she had time to do some work with Storm.

"Hello, boy," she said to Storm when she was back in the barn. "How are you feeling? Ready to go out?"

Storm looked calm and bright eyed, not at all tired by the weekend's competition. Amy led him out and gave him a quick brushing, then tacked him up and rode down to the training ring. She always made sure that the first training session after a show was a gentle one, and she began by taking him through the paces around the ring, gradually collecting him, then extending him, until his stride was flowing and easy. Storm didn't seem at all stiff after Saturday's exertions.

"Good boy," Amy praised him, bringing him back from a trot to a walk. She rode him around on a long rein, encouraging him to reach out and stretch his neck muscles. She saw Ty walking down to the ring and waved.

"Amy!" he called. "There's someone here to see you."

He needn't have called. Amy could see who it was. Ashley Grant had followed him down and was approaching the training ring. *I bet she's feeling smug,* Amy thought as she rode Storm over to the gate.

"So you did have my crop, after all," Ashley said with a smile.

"Yes. Sorry. It was a misunderstanding," said Amy stiffly. "Ben picked it up, and I found it in the trailer this morning."

She waited for Ashley's sarcastic comment, but it didn't come.

"Oh, no problem," said Ashley airily. "Like I said, I haven't been able to ride for the last couple of days. I see you're back on Storm."

"Yes," said Amy cautiously. Why wasn't Ashley rubbing it in? She slid down from Storm's back.

"Don't let me stop you from working," said Ashley hurriedly. "I'd be quite interested to see how you train him."

Amy gave a small smile. "Well, we're finished," she said.

Opening the training ring gate, she led Storm through.

Storm was calm, his ears pricked as they walked up to the stable yard. Amy expected Ashley to hurry off, but instead she sauntered alongside Storm, appraising him. "He looks relaxed," she commented. "Considering he's just had a workout."

Amy looked at her quickly and frowned. "Well, that was the idea," she said. "I'm easing him back into work after the show. How would you expect him to be?"

Ashley shrugged and said nothing. They reached the stable yard, and Amy looked at the other girl expectantly. Why was she hanging around like this? Amy's curiosity suddenly got the better of her. Ashley's visits were so out of character, even if she did have her crop as an excuse. She *had* to be after something. But what?

"So who's working Bright Magic while you're not riding?" she asked Ashley as she undid Storm's girth.

Ashley looked away, down the driveway. "My mother, I suppose," she said without looking at Amy.

"He was looking pretty wound up at the show," Amy went on.

"I don't need you to tell me that, thank you," said Ashley icily.

"I was only asking how he's doing," said Amy impatiently. "When are you going to start riding him again? You should be better soon."

Amy lifted the saddle off Storm's back and looked at

Ashley, who still kept her eyes averted. "Well, I won't be riding him," she said in an offhand voice.

"What?" Amy was amazed. "You won't be riding him? Why? The doctors said you'd be fine, didn't they?"

Ashley turned slowly to look at Amy. To Amy's complete astonishment, her lower lip was quivering, and her blue eyes had tears standing in them. "Bright Magic's been going badly for weeks," she confessed shakily. "Mom says it's my fault — that my riding's ruining him. She's training him herself, then she's going to find someone else to ride him in Jumpers classes."

Amy stared. She thought of the beautiful warmblood with his perfect conformation and giving face. And she thought of Val Grant riding him, pushing him until she'd squeezed all the generosity out of him. The thought made her angry. What a waste! For once, she found herself feeling sorry for Ashley — she couldn't help it. It was a strange feeling.

"So has he gotten any better since Saturday?" she asked.

"I don't know," said Ashley. She had quickly regained control of herself. "She won't let me near him."

Amy started walking toward the tack room with the saddle. "Well," she said, over her shoulder, "I'm not surprised he's been going badly, in that Kimblewick."

Ashley followed her and leaned against the door of the tack room as Amy settled the saddle onto its rack. "Do you really think it's the bit that's making a difference?" asked Ashley.

Amy shrugged. "Restrictive tack only deals with symptoms. It's never a cure," she said.

"Maybe I should try changing it," muttered Ashley, almost to herself.

Amy looked at her sharply. "I thought you said you weren't allowed to ride him."

A strange expression crossed Ashley's face. She looked anxious, determined, and rather secretive, all at once. She smoothed a perfect strand of hair behind one ear and faced Amy, looking her directly in the eye. "I have to figure this out," she said. "Bright Magic is *my* horse. I feel responsible for him. He was perfect when he first arrived, and I want to get him back to that. You know, Amy, he — he *deserves* it."

This was a big surprise for Amy. Ashley sounded as though she genuinely cared about Bright Magic. It was a side to the other girl that she hadn't seen before. From what Amy had seen, Ashley didn't relate to the horses she rode — she'd just had a string of perfect ponies without much character that did whatever they were told. But perhaps this horse was different.

"So what are you planning to do?" she asked Ashley warily as she picked up a grooming kit. She sneaked a look at Ashley as she did so. She still had that weird look of determination on her face.

"I'm going to ride him when my mom's not around," Ashley said. "I have to show her I can make the most of him. I don't want to lose him."

Amy walked back out onto the yard. She picked out a sweat scraper from the grooming kit and began to work over Storm's back in smooth sweeps. "What is your approach going to be?" she asked, giving Ashley a curious look.

Ashley smiled her bright, beautiful smile. "I was going to ask you that," she said. "To tell you the truth, I was wondering if you would help me."

Chapter Five

Amy almost dropped the sweat scraper in astonishment. Her mouth fell open. "*Help* you?" she questioned. "Help you with a horse?"

Ashley looked alarmed, and her expression hardened. "Well, maybe you want to think about it," she said hastily. "Could I have my crop now, please?"

Amy went to get it, still reeling in surprise. She didn't know whether to feel indignant or flattered by such an unexpected suggestion. She gave Ashley the crop and said good-bye without saying anything more about the proposition.

She was still mulling it over the next day when she and Soraya rode up toward Clairdale Ridge on Storm and Jasmine. Her friend was just as astonished at the news.

"Amazing," she exclaimed. "Ashley Grant eating humble pie. I never thought I'd live to see the day."

"Well, I wouldn't exactly say it was humble pie," Amy said uncertainly. "She might have asked me for help, but she was still pretty snarky about it."

"So what are you going to do?" demanded Soraya. "You're not going to help her, are you?"

Amy thought about it. More than anything, she thought about Bright Magic. She was sure that Ashley couldn't have had a personality transplant. But Bright Magic was a talented, sensitive horse, and Val Grant's harsh training was stifling him. And at the very least, Ashley had seemed genuinely concerned about him. She might not have completely changed her colors, but Bright Magic's refusal on Saturday had at least made her acknowledge that she wasn't always right.

Amy shrugged. "Ashley was pretty shaken up by her fall," she said. "I think it's made her realize she doesn't know everything."

"I guess," said Soraya doubtfully. "But Ashley's so selfish, Amy. And you'll be competing against her on Storm, remember."

"Oh, that," said Amy. "That doesn't worry me. Storm's going like a dream at the moment. Anyway, it's not really the point. Bright Magic is a talented horse that's being ridden the wrong way. I could make his life a whole lot easier."

Soraya looked hard at her, and Amy realized that her friend was reading her thoughts. "Amy," said Soraya. "You're already trying to figure out what's wrong with him, aren't you? You can't help yourself."

Amy grinned. They had reached an open stretch, and she pushed Storm into a canter. "I'm only thinking about it," she called back to Soraya. "That's all."

✇

Amy and Soraya clattered back to the stable yard just in time to see Ty's pickup entering the driveway.

"Hank!" exclaimed Amy. "I'd nearly forgotten. Soraya, could you cool down Storm for me? Ty and I need to take Hank to see Boxer."

"Sure, no problem," said Soraya, taking Storm's reins from Amy.

Amy waved to Ty, who was helping the old man out of the passenger side of his pickup. He was about seventy, and once he was out of the car, Amy could see that he had the same weather-beaten look as her grandfather. Hank was clearly a man who'd spent years outdoors.

Amy held out her hand. "Hello, Mr. Adams," she said politely. "I'm Amy. We spoke on the phone."

"Ah, there you are," said Hank. "I was wondering where you were."

Amy smiled and nodded, feeling puzzled by his greeting. "We'll take you down to the back barn," she said.

She looked over Hank's shoulder and saw Ty's face. He was looking worried. Amy raised an eyebrow questioningly, and, as Hank looked with interest at the stable block, he took her to one side.

"Amy, there's something wrong," he said in a low voice. "The trip here was totally weird. Meadowbridge is some kind of farm, I think. Hank was sitting outside, like he was waiting for me. I introduced myself and I said I'd come to take him to see Boxer, but I got the impression that he didn't remember making the plans. He said Ruth wasn't there, and then got in the car. But once we took off, Hank didn't seem to know where he was going. He started talking about Boxer and then about horses named Emerald and Snowy, as though I knew them. I think he's —"

Ty stopped talking when Hank turned toward them. "Things have changed a bit here, eh, Ruth?" he said to Amy.

"Um — yes, I suppose they have," she said. Then she added hesitantly, "It's Amy."

Hank nodded, stroking his chin. Amy couldn't be sure he'd taken in what she'd said. She exchanged glances with Ty, and they all started for the back barn. Hank strode along, looking around at the farm buildings.

They reached the barn, and Ty pulled open the door. Light flooded in, shafting down the aisle, and they stepped inside.

As they did so, they were greeted by a sudden, joyous whinny. The horse in the end stall peered over his half door, his eyes bright and his ears pricked. Amy gasped at the difference in Boxer. She turned to look at the old man's face, wondering what she would see, and the difference was astonishing. All the vagueness had gone. In its place was a beaming, radiant smile.

"Boxer!" cried the old man, rushing forward. "It's you, my old boy!"

Hank quickly let himself into Boxer's stall as Amy and Ty watched, astonished and delighted. Boxer nuzzled Hank's shoulder and snorted with joy. Hank scratched his neck and chortled, talking to the horse as though they'd never been parted.

"We should leave them alone for a while," said Ty. "But after the trip here, I really don't think —"

Ty stopped talking as Hank turned toward them. "Don't you worry about me, Ruth," he said to Amy. "Boxer will look after me, won't you, boy?"

He turned to the cob, who seemed to be almost quivering with joy. Amy stepped forward. "Mr. Adams," she said quietly, "I'm not Ruth, I'm Amy."

Hank looked at her doubtfully. Then he seemed to make a decision. He patted Boxer on the nose and said firmly, "You wait here, boy. I won't be long. We just have to do a quick check on the others. That's right, isn't it?"

He looked expectantly at Amy, who was dumbfounded.

Hank let himself out of the barn and made his way purposefully to the front yard once more, with Ty and Amy trailing after him anxiously. He stopped at Red's stall and leaned on the half door.

"Here, Sandy, boy," he called. Red peered around from munching on his hay net. "They're all doing fine," he said to Amy in a reassuring voice. "You can see that, can't you?" He patted her arm. "So don't you worry."

Amy didn't know what to say. She smiled at the old man, but inside she felt terribly concerned. No wonder Ruth had sounded so reluctant on the phone.

She turned, hearing a car. They weren't expecting anyone. The car came to a sudden halt, and a woman in her thirties stepped out. Her eyes were flashing, and she was clearly very angry. She marched up to Hank and took his arm.

It's Ruth Adams, Amy realized.

"Thank goodness you're OK," said Ruth to her father. Hank looked at her mildly, his face showing little comprehension. Ruth turned to Amy. "And *you*," she said, her voice almost shaking with fury, "must be Amy Fleming. How dare you take my father away like that, without telling me! Have you any *idea* how irresponsible you've been? You're lucky the caregiver saw the stable name on your truck, or else I would have called the police. How would I have known where he went?"

"Really, we didn't — " began Amy, stammering slightly, not knowing where to begin.

"It's not Amy's fault," cut in Ty.

Ruth rounded on him. "And who are *you*?" she stormed.

"I'm Ty Baldwin," said Ty calmly. "I'm Heartland's lead stable hand. I'm the one who picked up Hank. Amy called and spoke to Hank to arrange the visit. He seemed quite clear about it on the phone."

"Clear!" cried Ruth. "My father hasn't been *clear* about anything for years!"

"We realize our mistake now," said Amy, stepping forward. "Mr. Adams seems very confused about where he is. But we really had no idea, before today. You didn't tell us."

Ruth calmed down slightly and looked from Amy to Ty and back again. "Look, I should have said something," she said. "My father has Alzheimer's." She turned to the old man, who was looking toward the paddocks with a faraway look in his eyes. "He just isn't up to looking after horses anymore. He can't even look after himself. I'm sure you can see that. Sending Boxer away was for the best. If I knew more about horses, maybe I could have handled it, but I've never ridden one, let alone worked with them."

"I told you not to worry about Boxer," said Hank

brightly, cutting across Ruth. "We know what we're doing. He looks after me, you know."

Amy felt a wave of sadness sweep over her. The old man looked so sure about what he said, and he looked at their faces eagerly, expecting a response. Amy didn't know what to say. It was Ruth who stepped forward and took his arm. "Yes, I know, Daddy," she said quietly. "I'm not worrying about Boxer. I know everything's fine. Come on now. Let's get you home."

She steered the old man in the direction of her car and gently helped him into the passenger seat. Then she turned again to Ty and Amy. "I can't just keep bringing my father here. He's very confused. I was hoping that with Boxer gone, I'd have one less problem to deal with. That's the whole point, can't you see that?"

❧

"It seems so tragic," said Amy in a low voice as the car disappeared. "Imagine having to watch someone you love fade away like that."

"It's hard," agreed Ty with feeling. Something in the way he said it made Amy look at him quickly. His face was sad and thoughtful. "It's really scary when you feel you can't reach someone anymore," he added.

He knows, thought Amy. *His mother.* There must have been times when he had to watch her slide away into another world. Amy reached out and touched Ty's hand, and he gave her back a small smile.

"At least we know one thing," he said, taking her hand and squeezing it. "Boxer *is* pining for his owner."

Amy nodded. "We should check on him," she said as they walked down toward the back barn. But well before they reached it, they could hear the cob calling, his painful whinnies piercing the air. Amy rushed to open the barn door.

"Boxer," she said soothingly as she came to his stall.

The cob stood still, his ears pricked forward hopefully, his nostrils quivering. When he realized that it was only Ty and Amy at the door, he let out another shrill whinny of distress. He craned his neck over his half door to see beyond them into the yard.

"Boxer," murmured Amy, letting herself into his stall and stroking his neck. She looked up at Ty in despair. "What are we going to do with him, Ty?"

🙟

"What do you know about Alzheimer's, Grandpa?" asked Amy as she made herself a toasted cheese sandwich in the kitchen.

Grandpa was peeling potatoes at the sink. He turned, looking surprised. "That's a very serious question. Why?" he asked.

"It's Boxer's owner," Amy explained. "We've found out that he has Alzheimer's. That's why Boxer's been sent here."

"Oh," said Grandpa. "That's very sad." He stopped what he was doing and turned toward her, folding his arms. "An old friend of mine died of Alzheimer's. It creeps up very slowly on people. At first they think they're just getting a bit forgetful. Things we all do, all the time — like forget our keys or think we've left the iron on. But then it gets worse. Recent memories start to go, then past memories start getting muddled — people, places. The saddest time of all is when they don't recognize the people they're closest to. It's heartbreaking."

Amy thought of Ruth's face and nodded slowly. "I think Hank must be approaching the last stages," she said. "He thought I was Ruth, and the horses were all his." She frowned. "But he recognized Boxer," she said. "How could he do that? Get some things right and not others?"

"Perhaps he spent more time with Boxer than anyone else over the last few years," said Grandpa. "That might account for it. But in any case, it's a very unpredictable disease. You don't know which part of the memory is going to go next."

"Judging by Boxer's reaction to him, they were inseparable," said Amy. "I don't know how we're going to console him."

❧

Amy headed out into the late afternoon sun to tack up Storm. She thought he'd be ready to go over some more fences again, and she wanted to start preparing him for the next show. Feeling his springy, eager stride under her helped take her mind off Boxer's distress, and soon she had the gray gelding going well around the ring, concentrating on the job at hand.

When he was warmed up, she turned him toward the fences that she'd set up at one end of the ring. They weren't too high, but they were set at tricky angles to improve his agility and make him think.

"Now, turn!" urged Amy. Storm had just sailed over a brush fence, and she brought him around in a tight three-quarters turn to face the double. He tucked his hindquarters under him and kept his balance, taking only two short strides before taking off again.

"That's it!" said Amy. "And again!"

Storm cleared the second part of the double easily, and Amy clapped him on the neck with delight. She brought him back to a trot and waved at Lou, whom she'd spotted standing at the gate.

"Do you need me for something?" she called.

"No," called Lou. "Just watching. Keep going."

Amy rode Storm in a few wide, easy circles to cool

him off, then brought him over to where Lou was standing.

"Did you see us jumping?" she asked Lou.

Lou nodded. "He's looking great," she said. "It's not just his jumping. He's really balanced — turning on a dime."

"Yes," agreed Amy. "I think he's getting faster. We might even stand a chance of winning at the next show. I hope."

"I hope so, too," said Lou, but Amy caught a note of wistfulness in her voice. She remembered Lou asking to be involved in Storm's training. She knew it must be difficult for her, seeing Amy enjoy their father's gift so much. Impulsively, Amy had a thought.

"Lou, would you like to try riding him?" she asked. "You're really comfortable on Dancer now, and I've taken the edge off Storm's energy."

Lou hesitated, but her doubts were quickly replaced by excitement. "Do you really think I could?"

"Sure," said Amy. "He's so well schooled, Lou. Even if he were fresh, he'd listen to you."

Lou took a deep breath. "OK," she agreed.

Amy slid down from Storm's back as Lou let herself into the ring. Lou quickly mounted and Amy checked her stirrups. "I think you need them a hole longer," she said, making the changes. "Feel OK?"

Lou nodded and turned Storm to walk around the

ring. Amy watched, feeling suddenly anxious. Lou was riding on a tighter rein than Storm was used to. At the moment, though, he was still going forward willingly enough, and Amy resisted the urge to call out. She didn't want to interfere if she could help it.

When she was halfway around, Lou smiled and called over, "Is it OK if I try a trot?"

Amy nodded. "Go ahead!"

Lou gave Storm a firm nudge with her heels, and now Amy knew for certain that this had been a mistake. Lou had learned to ride as a child — she'd ridden sturdy, stubborn ponies that needed very obvious signals. She'd never made the transition to finely schooled horses like Storm. Storm was startled and plunged forward into a trot, slightly unseating Lou. She accidentally jabbed him in the mouth, and Storm tossed his head in protest. His trot became ragged, and in spite of her intentions, Amy started to shout instructions to her sister.

"Loosen up the reins, Lou!" she called. "Try to keep up his momentum; use your legs." But then, as Lou gave another firm nudge with her heels, Storm looked more confused than ever, and his trot became an unbalanced run around the ring. "Not your heels! He doesn't need it! He's not a pony." Amy bit her lip. The last thing she wanted was to sound patronizing, but it was too late.

Lou brought Storm back to a walk, and Amy ran over. "You're doing great, Lou. Just use your seat and your legs," said Amy. "He's really sensitive. He'll respond to shifts in your weight. When you ask him to trot, sit deep in the saddle and give a little squeeze. It's all he needs."

Lou nodded, her lips pursed, and set off once again around the ring. Amy watched critically. Now Lou was looking more tense, and Storm could sense it. "Relax your hands," called Amy. "Your wrists are stiff. They need to give more."

Instead, Lou pulled back and brought Storm to a halt. She sat, staring ahead, as Amy walked over.

"Are you OK?" asked Amy, looking up at her sister. Amy could see that Lou was biting her lip, and her eyes looked glassy. She was fighting back tears. "Lou, I'm sorry — I didn't mean to —"

"It's OK," said Lou, getting a grip on herself again. She took her feet out of the stirrups and dismounted. She handed Storm's reins to Amy. "I guess I'm just not ready," she said quietly.

"Lou —" began Amy, but her sister was already walking away to the edge of the ring, her head bowed in disappointment.

Amy stroked Storm's nose, thinking. Life could be so unfair. It was Lou who had wanted to find their father again, Lou who had been to England to look for him, Lou who had insisted that Amy meet him again even though Amy had been resigned not to. But when they had all been reunited, it was the love of horses and riding that had brought Amy and her father together. And Lou had struggled to find common ground with him.

And then there had been the gift of Storm. Amy knew that Lou had been disappointed that their father had thought more about Amy than about her in buying the jumper. But only now, seeing her dejected figure reach the gate, did she see quite *how* disappointed. Why hadn't she seen it before? Did their father have any idea how thoughtless he had been?

Chapter Six

"Hello, boy. How are you doing?" murmured Amy, slipping into Boxer's stall. The cob's head was hanging low, and Amy's shoulders sagged in despair. She stood back and assessed the cob's condition. His coat was thinning, and she could see his ribs. He was definitely getting weaker. She stroked his neck and felt the roughness of it.

"No change?" asked Ty, looking over the stall door.

"No," said Amy. She picked up the bucket that stood in one corner of the stall. "I gave him another wormwood infusion earlier, but he hasn't touched it."

She felt tears pricking at the back of her eyes. Seeing the dejection in every line of Boxer's body was hard to bear. And it brought back such sad memories. Pegasus had looked just the same before he'd died.

"Come on," said Ty gently. "You need to eat. We'll check on him again later."

Amy nodded and let herself out of the stall. They walked to the farmhouse together. It was Wednesday evening and time for the weekly dinner meeting. Amy wasn't looking forward to it. She hated having to say that a horse wasn't getting better — mainly, of course, because she felt so bad for the horse. But when she couldn't make any difference, she was also reminded of Marion. She had learned everything she knew from her mother, and she still longed for her advice at times like this.

"We had two more phone calls today," said Lou when everyone was sitting around the kitchen table. "That means we have a waiting list of five. But I guess nothing's changed since last week?"

"Well," said Ty, "Dancer is pretty much ready to go to new owners. She's fully recovered. She's put on all the weight she'd lost, and she's used to everyone riding her. She could easily be rehomed now."

Ty's words were true, but Amy felt terrible. Dancer was the one horse that Lou felt comfortable riding — the gentle paint mare had helped her to overcome her fears, and she was always the horse that Lou rode out on the trails. Amy shot her a glance. Lou's face was still.

"If she's ready to go, then she should go," Lou said. "I'll start looking for someone who would be a good match for her."

Amy concentrated on her supper. This week, no one mentioned the obvious — that Storm was taking up a stall that could be used for a horse that needed help.

The subject of Dancer closed, Ty brought up the problem of Boxer. "It's clear now that he's missing his owner, but Ruth Adams has said that Hank can't visit again. It's difficult to know what we can do," he said.

"Boxer's health is deteriorating fast," said Amy heavily. "There's no way he can go to a new owner yet. He needs our care. I'm sorry, Lou."

"I understand," said Lou with a faint smile. "You were right — there's a lot more to Boxer's situation than we knew at first."

A lot more, thought Amy. But unfortunately, knowing more wasn't making Boxer's life any easier.

That night, Amy lay awake thinking about Hank. Her heart filled with sadness at the memory of the old man's confusion and his obvious joy at seeing his old friend. *What would it be like to lose your mind like that? Did Hank know what was happening to him?* From what Grandpa had said, he must have known for a while — when he first realized he was becoming forgetful. Everything was probably jumbled up now. Only the strongest memories still meant anything.

The strongest memories, thought Amy. How strange, she

reflected, that his own daughter, Ruth, was becoming confused in Hank's mind, but not Boxer. Was it just a coincidence? Or was there something about his relationship with Boxer that could explain why those memories were so vivid, so true? If there was, perhaps there was something about it that could help Boxer come to terms with his loss.

Suddenly, Amy felt a rush of frustration with Ruth. Why was she being so unhelpful? Couldn't she see the strength of the bond between her father and his horse? Would it really be so difficult to let them see each other occasionally? She thought back once more to the image of Hank greeting Boxer in his stall and the horse's whinny of joy. It was a moment of clarity for both of them.

But if Ruth held her ground and refused to allow Hank to visit, what hope was there? Amy's heart filled with despair. She thought again of Pegasus and how he had faded away to his death. Tears pricked at the back of her eyes at the memory of it. And of Sugarfoot — how desperately weak he'd become.

But that thought gave her hope. Sugarfoot hadn't died. He had found the will to live again. By singing to him, Lou had unintentionally found the thing that had reminded him of his owner and given him hope. It had brought back some happiness, and the pony's strength had gradually returned. And perhaps Hank could offer something — some key that would point Amy in the right direction. He knew Boxer better than anyone. She had to speak to him at least one more time. She needed one more chance to help both Boxer and Hank.

℮

The next morning, Amy woke with a new sense of purpose. After coffee with Matt, she would go to Meadowbridge and try to talk to Hank. There had to be a way to move forward. She checked the directions with Ty. It would be easy enough to get there by bus.

"Going somewhere special?" Lou asked as Amy pulled her sweater off its hook.

"I'm meeting Matt in town for coffee," said Amy. "Then I'm going to Meadowbridge to see if I can find out anything that would help Boxer. You know, the Adamses' place."

"Well, good luck," said Lou. Then she raised an eyebrow. "You haven't seen Matt for ages," she commented.

"No," said Amy. She made a face. "Thanks to Ashley."

"Well, say hi to him from me," said Lou.

"I'll do that," said Amy. "See you later."

It was true, thought Amy as she walked down the drive, *that Matt's relationship with Ashley had changed things*. Less than six months ago, Matt and Amy had been close friends. Around the holidays Matt had asked Amy out, and she'd said she didn't feel the same way. They decided to stay friends. Shortly after that, Matt had started dating Ashley.

Amy climbed into the bus to town, wondering what Matt had to tell her. Maybe it was Ashley — they were always splitting up and getting back together. Whatever had happened between them, she doubted it would last long.

Matt was waiting for her in Jerry's when she arrived. She smiled and waved.

"Long time no see," she said, sitting down opposite him.

Matt looked a bit embarrassed. "I guess," he said.

Amy ordered a chocolate milk shake and a blueberry muffin. "I'm starving," she said. "I had breakfast hours ago."

"No sleeping in, even on vacation?" Matt smiled.

"I work with horses, remember," Amy said playfully, punching his arm. She took a bite out of the muffin. "So," she said, looking hard at Matt. "How are things?"

Matt gave her a wry look. "There's no need to be polite, Amy, it's just me," he said. "Go ahead and ask the real question."

"OK," said Amy cautiously. "You and Ashley broke up again. Didn't you?"

"Yes," acknowledged Matt, sighing.

"I'm sorry," said Amy sympathetically. There was no point in saying she thought it was for the best. She'd done that before, and then they'd gotten back together. "Maybe she'll change her mind again."

"What makes you think it was her decision?" asked Matt indignantly.

"It wasn't?" said Amy.

Matt looked exasperated. "No, as a matter of fact, it wasn't," he said. "It was mine. I got sick of her moods, her being supernice and then really rude without warning. I decided it was a waste of energy. I don't want to go out with someone who doesn't really like me."

Amy blushed. She couldn't be sure he was talking about her refusing to go out with him, but it sounded like his words had a double meaning. "No, you shouldn't do that," she said. Quickly, she changed the subject. "You know, Ashley's been to Heartland a couple of times recently," she offered.

"To Heartland?" Matt looked astonished.

"Yeah, she wants me to help her with her new horse," Amy finished.

If Amy had said that Ashley had grown another head, Matt couldn't have looked more surprised. He leaned back in his seat and stared at her. "Ashley wants you to help her?" he repeated wonderingly.

"That's what she says," agreed Amy.

"And are you going to?" asked Matt incredulously.

"I'm thinking about it," admitted Amy. "Bright Magic needs help. He's having a bad time with Val Grant.

And to be honest, Ashley seems pretty desperate about it all."

Matt stirred his latte with a spoon, then drank some. "Well," he said thoughtfully, "there's probably no one who needs help more than Ashley."

Now it was Amy's turn to be surprised. "What do you mean?" she questioned.

Matt looked at Amy frankly. "Ashley Grant is one of the most unhappy people I know," he said. "Her mother rules her with a rod of iron. Whenever she puts a foot wrong, her life isn't worth living. Sure, she has designer clothes, blond hair, and flashy horses. But she doesn't have what you have. She doesn't have good people around her, and she doesn't have anything decent to live for, anything she really believes in. Her whole life revolves around keeping her mother off her back."

Amy reflected on how different Matt's impression of Ashley was from the one that Ashley always shared with the world. "You know, Amy," Matt continued, "I tried really hard with her. I really *cared* for her. But there's only so much you can give when you're going out with someone. Ashley needs help, and I'm not the right person to give it to her, not if she's not willing to take it."

"Well, I might not be the right person, either," Amy said hesitantly.

Matt put his head to one side and shrugged. "I wouldn't really know," he said. "But think of it this way.

You and Ashley have never exactly been friends. It must have cost her a lot of pride, asking you to help."

"I guess so," said Amy slowly. She toyed with her milk shake straw, thinking. She had been considering saying yes to Ashley for the horse's sake. But now she had some sympathy for Ashley, too. "Thanks, Matt," she added. "You've helped me make up my mind."

After waving good-bye to Matt outside Jerry's, Amy walked to the bus stop for Davidstown. The bus would drop her near enough to Meadowbridge. As she sat watching the Virginia countryside pass by, she thought about what Matt had said. Not just about Ashley, but about herself as well. How she was surrounded by people who loved her, and how she had something good to live for. Her heart warmed at the thought of Ty, Lou, and Grandpa and the work they all did at Heartland. If she didn't have all that, what would life be like?

Amy got off the bus and walked the half mile to Meadowbridge. When she turned into the drive, she felt surprised. Ty had said it was some kind of farm, and she had imagined a small operation. She hadn't expected this — an immense pasture, with a large farmhouse in one corner. It was clearly a sizable farm that had seen better days. Wisps of straw had drifted up into corners of the barn doorways. There didn't seem to be any animals around, and the whole place had a slightly desolate air. A car was parked outside the farmhouse, but it wasn't the one that Ruth had arrived in. Amy figured it must belong to the caregiver. She went up to the front door and knocked.

A large woman came to the door. She was in her forties and tall, with a sensitive, kind-looking face. Amy quickly explained that she was the person looking after Hank's old horse, Boxer.

"And I'm Martha," said the woman. "I'm here looking after Hank. Ruth's at work."

"Would it be possible for me to speak to him?" Amy asked.

Martha looked dubious. Amy could tell from the shrewd look in her eyes that she was appraising her carefully. "You know, he doesn't understand much these days," she said.

"I know that," said Amy quietly. "But he still remembers Boxer, doesn't he?"

"Sure, he does," said Martha. "Though whether he makes much sense of what he remembers is another thing."

"I'd appreciate just a few minutes with him," said Amy.

To Amy's relief, she seemed to have met with Martha's approval. Martha nodded and stepped to one side. "That should be OK," she said. "Come on in."

Amy followed her into a spacious open-plan kitchen. "Can I get you a drink?" asked Martha, going to the big walk-in fridge. "Some orange juice or something?"

Amy smiled and shook her head. "I'm fine, thanks. I won't be staying long."

Martha poured herself a juice. "I should probably tell you that talking about Boxer might put him in touch with some real memories," she said. "And that can be distressing. But it's not necessarily a bad thing."

"Why would it be distressing?" asked Amy, puzzled.

Martha sighed. "People with Alzheimer's can get very agitated when they realize what's happening to them. In the early and intermediate stages, it's particularly hard. They know they're losing their minds — imagine what it's like to have to deal with that. Later on, they're not so aware of it. Ignorance is bliss, as they say."

"So reminding him of Boxer may remind him of what's really happening?" said Amy slowly.

"But it's not right to shield people from everything," Martha continued. "It might be upsetting, but remembering Boxer also helps Hank hold on to who he is. It helps him maintain his dignity, you know?" She lowered her voice. "If you ask me, it's a real shame the horse had to go."

Amy looked at Martha enquiringly. "Really? Why do you say that?"

Martha opened her mouth to speak, then changed her

mind and shook her head. "It's not for me to say," she said.

"Please," said Amy. "I'm trying to understand what's happening to Boxer. Anything you can tell me might help."

Martha pursed her lips. Amy could see she was choosing her words thoughtfully. "I'm not judging," she said. "Ruth's had a tough time, and she's done her best. But with Boxer . . ."

"What happened?" asked Amy.

"There were difficult decisions to be made," said Martha. "There was no one to look after Boxer, other than herself. So she decided he had to go. Otherwise, she would have had to get someone in to clean the stable and feed him."

"And you think she should have done that?"

"Like I said, it's not for me to say, and I'm not judging her," said Martha. "But Boxer was Hank's last hold on the real world. Ruth couldn't seem to see it. She said she had enough to deal with — and she has had a lot. . . ." She trailed off. "Come on, I'll take you to Hank. He's sitting out back in the sun."

Martha walked briskly out of the kitchen, and Amy followed her through the house to an open veranda. Hank was sitting in a wicker chair, rocking gently.

"Someone to see you, Hank," said Martha cheerily. "She's come to talk about Boxer."

"Boxer! Is he here?" asked the old man eagerly, struggling to get to his feet.

"No, no, you stay where you are," said Martha soothingly. "She's only come to talk about him."

"What's happened to Boxer?" asked Hank, anxiety filling his voice. "You let me see him, I'll make sure he's all right —"

"He's not here, Hank," repeated Martha. "Boxer's fine. I meant she's looking after him, like you used to."

Hank stared at Martha blankly for a moment, then relaxed slightly and peered at Amy. She sat down in the chair next to him and smiled. Martha picked up the lunch tray from the table next to Hank and nodded at her. "I'll leave you to it," she said. "Just call me if you need anything."

"Thanks," said Amy. She drew her chair nearer to Hank's and took a deep breath. This wasn't going to be easy. "Hank, I'm Amy," she began. "Do you remember? I'm looking after Boxer at Heartland. You came to visit us there."

Hank smiled and patted her hand. "You're a good girl," he said. "I know you're working hard."

"Yes," agreed Amy. "We're doing our best with Boxer. He misses you."

"Now, don't you worry about Boxer. You have enough to worry about," responded Hank.

"Well, yes," said Amy. "But we're looking after Boxer, just the same."

"No, no," Hank persisted in a reassuring tone. "You leave Boxer to me. All those books, they're enough for you to be thinking about. I always said that education's the thing. Education's the thing."

Amy stared at him, baffled. Once more, Hank seemed to be confusing her with Ruth. It was clearly no use trying to tell him otherwise — she might as well go along with it and see what she could learn.

"Yes, I know my education's important," she said slowly. "That's what you want for me, isn't it?"

Hank smiled gently. "I always said the farm wouldn't be enough for you. You'll go on to better things," he said. "I always said we'd manage, and we do that, we do that. Sure we do."

Amy thought quickly. "Who's *we*?" she asked carefully. "Who will manage?"

Hank shook his head impatiently. "Me and Boxer," he said, as though it were obvious. "That's right. Me and Boxer, we'll take care of the others. We'll take care of them. There's no need for you to be worrying your head about them."

Amy was having difficulty following again. Who were *they*? The others?

"How will you take care of them?" she asked. "What do you and Boxer do?"

Hank spread his hands out in front of him and counted carefully with one finger on the palm of his other hand as he spoke. "Well, we'll get up early in the morning. We'll get down to the open fields. We'll check them all over. We'll bring them in, every one of them. Every one of them. Every day. So don't you worry."

"That's good," murmured Amy. "That's good."

"You understand now?" said Hank. "It upsets me to see you worry. It's all for the best, my girl, I can tell you that. You'll thank me later. You will."

Hank stopped talking and turned to gaze out over the fields. The rays of afternoon sun caught his face, and he blinked slowly. Amy sat quietly, too, thinking. Whatever Hank had done in his life, it hadn't been easy. But Hank hadn't wanted Ruth to worry. He'd wanted her to get a good education. *But why is he so concerned about Ruth,* Amy wondered. Didn't Hank have a wife? Did Ruth have a mother? Whoever she had been, she clearly wasn't around anymore.

More important, she wondered who *they* were — who did Hank and Boxer check over early in the morning? Meadowbridge must have been a working farm, but what kind? Hank had mentioned other horses, but that was all.

"Who do you look after with Boxer?" she asked. "What kind of farming do you do?"

Hank smiled indulgently. "You ask a lot of questions,"

he replied. "Don't you bother yourself with that. You get back to your schoolbooks."

Amy realized that Hank had slipped back into his familiar refrain and that there wasn't much point in continuing. His wrinkled face looked exhausted. She stood up.

"Martha!" she called softly.

Martha appeared swiftly in the doorway. "Are you OK?" she asked.

"Fine," said Amy. "But I think I should leave now."

Martha came over. She bent down and took Hank's hand. "Do you want to rest now?" she asked him gently.

The old man's eyes gazed at her unseeingly. Amy could see that he had withdrawn into himself. He had gone, for the time being.

Martha straightened up. "I think I'd better see to him," she said to Amy in a low voice. "Can you let yourself out?"

"Of course," said Amy. "Thank you for letting me speak to him. And thanks for talking to me, too." She leaned forward and took Hank's other hand. "Bye, Hank," she said softly. But if the old man heard, he showed no sign of it.

❧

Back outside, Amy decided to have a quick look around. She followed the driveway around the side of the house and was surprised to see a whole series of livestock sheds. The front yard had several, but now Amy could see that Meadowbridge had taken a lot of looking after in its day. She peered into one big, long barn and saw rows of milking stalls. So it had been a dairy farm. And not a small one, either.

Amy wondered how many horses there had been. She went back to the front yard, where she had seen what looked like stables. There was a row of four stalls, but as soon as Amy looked over their half doors, she could see that most of them had not been occupied by a horse for a long time. One was stacked high with straw, while another two were cluttered with pieces of farm machinery. Only the end one looked as though it had been used recently. Amy inspected it closely. Its floor was still lined with thick straw bedding, and there was a manger in one corner. Just like any horse's stall. Amy fingered the bolt on the door, staring into the empty space. There was nothing much to glean from it. She headed off down the driveway.

Sitting in the bus on the way back to Heartland, Amy pondered what she had learned. It was as though Hank was stuck, like a needle on an old record, playing the same refrain in his head, over and over again. She wondered if he did that all the time or just when he saw Amy. Perhaps she reminded him of a particular time in his life — when Ruth had been about her age, or a bit older. It was impossible to know for sure. What *did* seem clear, though, was that he had been determined to do the best for his daughter at any cost. And Boxer? Boxer, Amy guessed, had helped to keep him going. Boxer was a constant companion.

Then Amy thought about Ruth. Ruth was much more difficult to understand. She had sent Boxer to Heartland, even though, as Martha had said, Boxer was Hank's last tie to reality. Why would she do such a thing? Was it just about money? Or was it an issue of time, as Martha had suggested? Hank gave the impression that he'd been a devoted father. Why would Ruth want to take away the one thing that still meant something to him? Amy found the whole situation baffling.

She found her mind drifting to Tim, her own father. He had never been there for Amy, worrying about her future, telling her what she needed to do, supporting her through thick and thin. He hadn't been there at all. Until this year, she'd just thought of him as the man who'd abandoned her mother. When she'd finally met him again, it had taken Amy quite a while to understand that he had only left his wife because he couldn't cope with his injuries. He had never stopped loving his daughters. But it must be very different for Ruth. She could never have doubted her father's love — could she?

The thoughts churned around Amy's head as the bus

rolled toward Heartland. She felt frustrated, and when she got off the bus she wondered if her visit had been worth the effort. She wasn't any nearer to helping Boxer.

As she walked up the driveway, she suddenly heard voices calling her urgently. She looked in the direction of the house. Ty and Lou were running toward her, waving their arms.

"What is it?" Amy exclaimed, breaking into a jog to meet them. "What's happened?"

"Amy!" gasped Lou. "Thank goodness you're here. Boxer's gone!"

Chapter Seven

"Gone!" Amy stared at them. "What do you mean, *gone*?"

"I was just sweeping the aisle in the barn," explained Ty. "And I saw Boxer's door was ajar. I asked Ben if he'd turned him out, but he hadn't. He's not in the paddock."

"But how could he get out?" asked Amy as all three of them hurried back toward the yard.

"The bolt was undone," said Ty helplessly. "But I don't know how."

They reached the yard, and Grandpa came to meet them.

"I've checked all the buildings around the yard," he told them, looking worried. "I think the best thing is for us to spread out and check every part of the property systematically."

Amy thought quickly. "Grandpa," she asked, "are there any cattle grazing near here?"

Jack Bartlett looked puzzled. "Abram Marsh has a small herd. They'd be just beyond the outer fields, over by the creek. Why? What's that got to do with it?"

"It's just a hunch," said Amy. "I'm going to check in that direction."

She headed out behind the stable yard to the meadows beyond. She ran along the track toward the outer meadows until she was aching. Slowing to a walk, she shielded her eyes against the sun and scanned the fields ahead. There, to the left, beyond Heartland's fields, was the small herd of cattle. And they weren't grazing. They were staring at something, something that was out of Amy's sight. She broke into a jog again and rounded the next bend in the track. Then she stopped dead.

Boxer was standing with his head over the fence, staring at the cattle. They seemed to stare back. Amy approached him softly, anxious not to startle him.

"Boxer," she whispered.

Boxer turned his head and saw her but didn't move. He simply looked back toward the cattle and whickered softly. The cattle eyed him suspiciously, sniffing the air and blowing through their soft nostrils. Amy walked forward slowly, getting closer and closer. Boxer still didn't move to escape her. She stepped up to his head and gently grasped his halter.

"Hey, boy," she soothed. "You had us all worried."

She scratched his nose and looked at his calm, peaceful gaze. The only time she had seen him looking this happy was when Hank had visited. She gave his halter a little tug.

"Come on," she said regretfully. "I can't leave you here. We need to tell the others you're all right."

Boxer didn't resist. As Amy led him to the yard, there was an unexpected lightness in her heart. Perhaps there was hope for Boxer after all — hope and a purpose.

🐝

Amy led Boxer back to the barn. She bolted him into his stall again and hurried to find the cell phone in her bag. Quickly, she punched in Grandpa's number.

"I've found him!" she told her grandfather when he answered. "I'll call the others and let them know."

"That's good news!" said Grandpa, sounding relieved. "I'll see you up at the house."

Twenty minutes later, Ty and Lou had joined Grandpa and Amy at the kitchen table for some celebratory coffee and cookies.

"So where was he?" asked Lou.

Amy explained about her visit to Meadowbridge. Jack Bartlett, who understood more about farming than any of them, listened intently.

"Dairy farming is no joke," he commented when Amy

had finished. "It's an exhausting life. Dairy cattle are like children. You can't leave them to their own devices for even half a day. They have to be milked and tended to all day. And if the farm was as big as you say . . ."

"I got the impression it had been huge at one time — before Hank became sick," said Amy. "He must have had more horses, but not for some time. Boxer's stall was the only one that looked like it had been used recently."

"Maybe he didn't have much hired help," said Grandpa. "He and Boxer might have kept the whole thing running between them."

"That's the impression I got from Hank," agreed Amy. "He seems to remember the names of other horses from time to time, but mostly he just talks about himself and Boxer and how they would manage it all. They must have been inseparable."

"A real working team." Grandpa nodded. "Well, it certainly explains why Boxer headed for the cattle. They were what he lived for. That was what bonded him to Hank."

"But what it doesn't explain," observed Lou, "is why Ruth was so set on moving Boxer to Heartland. Or why she won't let Hank visit. I would think it would be good for him to see his old horse every once in a while."

"That's what the caregiver hinted at," agreed Amy. "She said that Ruth couldn't look after Boxer anymore — but she suggested that it was possible if she'd really wanted to."

"So it all comes back to Ruth," said Ty thoughtfully.

"It seems like that's the case," said Amy.

A silence fell around the table briefly.

"I tell you what we haven't thought about," said Lou suddenly. "How did Boxer get out in the first place? It's doubtful that someone would have left his door unbolted. Could he have slipped the bolt back himself?"

Amy and Ty exchanged looks of alarm. Of course. Some horses did learn to fiddle with the lock and open it. And Amy had a sudden memory of playing with the bolt at Meadowbridge. It hadn't been a straightforward slipping bolt. It had an extra catch attached. "I'd better go and check," said Ty, getting to his feet hurriedly.

"I'll come with you," said Amy.

❧

To their relief, Boxer was still in his stall, standing with his back to the door. Ty examined the bolt.

"It's difficult to tell whether he opened it himself," he said. "But we'd better add an extra catch to the bolt, just in case."

"We could secure it with some string for now," suggested Amy. "Then we'd better keep an eye on him, to see if he's fiddling with it."

"I'll work it out," said Ty.

"Thanks," said Amy, smiling and giving him a quick

peck on the cheek. "I'm going to do a session with Dylan before it gets too late."

She went to the tall bay horse's stall. He had an unusual problem — he was very clumsy. When he'd first arrived, it was as though he didn't know where his feet were. Amy and Ty had been working on his coordination and had made a maze of poles for him to walk over. He'd shown great improvement, but he wasn't ready to go back to his owner.

Amy concentrated on guiding him around the ring, watching his feet carefully for half an hour. It was only when she led him back to the yard, with the shadows lengthening and the sun low in the sky, that she realized how tired she was. It had been a long day; it seemed hours since she'd sat with Matt in Jerry's, drinking her milk shake.

Thinking of Matt reminded her — she had to call Ashley and talk to her about Bright Magic. She made sure Dylan was settled and went inside.

&

"You look exhausted," commented Lou when Amy came in. "Was Boxer OK?"

"Fine — for now. Still in his stall, at least," said Amy. "And yes, I think I've had it for today. But I need to call Green Briar before I forget."

"To talk to Daniel?" asked Lou.

Amy shook her head. "Ashley, actually." Lou raised an eyebrow, and Amy grinned. "I know what you're thinking," she added. "But Matt helped me to see her in a new light."

"Really? And what kind of light would that be?" queried Lou. "A bright red warning beacon, I hope."

"Very funny, Lou," Amy replied. "Not this time. I'm going to trust that she wants what's best for her horse."

"Good luck," said Lou as Amy picked up the phone. She dialed the Green Briar number, hoping desperately that it wouldn't be Val who answered. To her relief, she heard Ashley's voice.

"Hi, Ashley," she said tentatively. "It's Amy."

"Amy!" said Ashley sweetly. "How nice of you to call."

"I was calling about Bright Magic."

"Oh, what about him?" Ashley sounded light and off-hand.

"How is he?" asked Amy. "Have you been working with him?"

"My mom has," said Ashley. "But I thought I'd wait to hear from you before trying anything myself."

Ashley's words sounded sugar sweet, and Amy felt instantly irritated. She couldn't imagine Ashley hanging around waiting for her under any circumstances. But she remembered Matt's words and controlled herself. "Well, I'd like to help, if you want me to," she said, trying to sound gracious about it.

"Oh, Amy, that's great," exclaimed Ashley, and Amy had to admit to herself that she sounded genuinely pleased. Then Ashley dropped her voice to a conspiratorial whisper. "Could you come over tomorrow morning? Mom's away all day, so she won't notice if Bright Magic's a bit tired."

Amy was taken aback. It felt as though Ashley had thought it all through already — but how could she have known that Amy would say yes? Again, she bit her lip. "I'm not sure," she answered calmly. "I'll need to find someone to bring me over. I'll let you know."

"Don't worry about that, Amy," said Ashley hastily. "I'll send a driver over for you."

Amy's irritation grew. She didn't feel like fitting into Ashley's neat little plan. "It's not just the drive over, Ashley," she said frostily. "I'll need to rearrange my work as well. Like I said, I'll let you know."

"Well, please don't let me down, Amy," said Ashley. "I've been really counting on your help. I think you're Magic's only hope."

Now Amy was truly disconcerted. Surely Ashley couldn't mean all this stuff. But again, there was something in her voice that sounded genuine. "I'll do my best," she found herself saying.

"Thank you. Speak to you soon," Ashley said quickly and then hung up the phone.

🙟

"You want to go *where*?" exclaimed Ty when she explained the situation to him.

Amy felt awkward. Ty wasn't into shows at the best of times. For him, the work at Heartland had nothing to do with winning competitions. She remembered how he'd felt about her helping Daniel with Amber, before he'd realized Daniel's situation and how much had depended on his next show. And now Amy was agreeing to help with another show horse — *Ashley*'s show horse!

"Ty, I know it's not your thing," she said. "If it weren't summer vacation, I wouldn't even consider it. But I do have a bit more time at the moment, and, well, Bright Magic really needs some help."

Ty shook his head wryly. "Amy Fleming, you will never cease to amaze me," he said. "OK. I'll take you over to Green Briar. I've got to go that way, anyway. I'm taking the afternoon off."

The next day, Amy spent the morning doing the usual chores, then she did a quick training session with Storm and some T-touch on Dylan before joining Ty in his pickup.

"I checked on Boxer's door this morning," said Ty as they left Heartland. "He's been chewing at the string. So it looks like it's possible that he let himself out yesterday."

Amy frowned. "Well, that problem was solved easily enough," she said. "But Ruth should have told us he pulls stunts like that."

"Sounds like she wouldn't have known," said Ty gently. "She didn't have much to do with the horses, remember? So if the door at Meadowbridge had a special catch, she wouldn't have even questioned why."

"I guess," said Amy grudgingly. Lou had made them sandwiches. She unwrapped them and handed one to Ty.

"Thanks," said Ty. They ate in silence for a few minutes.

"You really don't . . . *like* Ruth much, do you?" asked Ty suddenly.

Amy shot him a sharp glance. "What do you mean?" she asked indignantly. The question of liking people she helped wasn't really an issue as far as Amy was concerned. Or she didn't think it was. If a horse needed help, that often meant helping a person, too. But Heartland couldn't pick and choose *who*. After all, here she was on her way to help Ashley, of all people.

"You think she's treated Hank badly by sending Boxer to Heartland. She doesn't understand the relationship between people and horses. So you don't like her," said Ty. "Am I right?"

Amy felt slightly horrified at Ty's words. She thought about it. Maybe he was right. She didn't warm to Ruth, and the more she found out about Hank and Boxer, the more she didn't see why Hank should be kept away from his old friend. And she had to acknowledge that Hank's devotion to his daughter had aroused a flash of — something. Envy? She couldn't be sure.

"I — don't know," she said cautiously.

"Have you considered that Ruth might be feeling guilty?" asked Ty quietly.

"Guilty?" asked Amy in astonishment. "No. Why would she feel that?"

Ty frowned thoughtfully. "When your parents have problems, you can start to blame yourself, even if it's not your fault," he said. "And if you have to look after them, feelings of resentment can creep in, too. You don't *want* to feel like that, and you know you shouldn't. So you end up feeling guilty about it."

Something in the way Ty said this made Amy stare at him with curiosity. She wondered if what Ty was saying reflected his own experience. "Ty," she asked tentatively, "do you say that because you feel guilty about your mother?"

Ty hesitated. "Well — I guess," he confessed. "I wish I didn't. I can't help it. Dad always hated me working with horses. He thinks they're just toys for rich people. Whenever he gives me a hard time about it, Mom gets all wound up. It makes her worse. So I feel like it's my fault that she's depressed, or at least that I don't make things any easier for her. That's why I try to do as much as I can to help her out."

"But it's never enough?" asked Amy softly.

"No. She never really gets any better. It just goes in cycles. But then again, I never stop working with horses."

"How could you?" exclaimed Amy. "You have a gift with horses."

"Yeah," agreed Ty sadly. "I like to think about it that way, but my mom and dad see it differently."

Amy looked out the window. Now it was her turn to feel guilty. Ty carried all this around with him, and she'd never known. She felt terrible. "So is that why you don't want me to visit?" she said in a low voice. "Bringing home someone from Heartland will only make things worse?"

Ty nodded. "Something like that," he agreed awkwardly. He sighed. "It's just that Mom gets pretty anxious about stuff. I don't want to add to that."

"Ty, I'm really sorry," said Amy. "I've never asked you about your family. And I'm sorry you've had to deal with it all on your own."

"It's OK," said Ty. "If I'd needed your help, I would have asked you. You know that. Like I've told you — when I'm at Heartland, I want to concentrate on the work there. It's easier that way."

"That makes sense," said Amy. "I understand now, about not visiting. Let's forget about it."

Ty smiled and reached for her hand. "Thanks," he said simply.

🙚

They reached the gates of Green Briar, and Amy unbuckled her seat belt.

"Just drop me off here. I'll walk up," she said. "See you tomorrow."

"Good luck," said Ty as Amy got out of the pickup.

Amy walked up the perfectly maintained driveway to the main stable yard. Horses grazed in neat little paddocks on either side. Now that she was here, Amy wondered what she was doing. She hated this place. But she barely had time to think about it, because Ashley was waiting for her, with Bright Magic already tacked up.

"Hi, Amy." Ashley smiled. As usual, she looked immaculate in breeches and a crisp white button-down. "I got one of the grooms to tack up Bright Magic for me. I'm afraid he's going to be a little fresh."

Amy looked at Magic's proud, powerful head. Even though no one had mounted him yet, he was restless and played constantly with the harsh Kimblewick bit. Amy stroked his neck, soothing him.

"First of all, let's change his tack," she said. "You used to ride him in a snaffle, didn't you? I thought you were going to go back to that."

"I thought about that, yes," said Ashley hastily. "But

it's really not a good idea. You can't do anything with him in a snaffle. He ignores you."

Amy pursed her lips. "It looks like you can't do anything with him in a Kimblewick, either," she pointed out. "If I'm going to work with him, I'd like you to change his bit back to a snaffle. And change the martingale to a running one — or for that matter, take it off altogether. I don't think he needs one."

Ashley looked slightly surprised at this but did as Amy suggested. When Bright Magic was back in his old tack, they led him out to the training rings. Usually, Ashley liked nothing better than to point out how much bigger and better the riding facilities were at Green Briar than at Heartland — more training rings, more stables, more of everything. But today she quietly led Bright Magic to the smallest ring and opened the gate.

"Ride him around a little so we can see how he's going," suggested Amy when they were inside.

Ashley looked alarmed. "But I thought you were going to work with him," she said. "I'm not riding him in this tack. He'll go crazy."

"The point isn't just to work with Bright Magic," said Amy. "It's not as if it's his problem alone. Horses don't start going badly on their own. I can't just *fix* Bright Magic and hand him back to you."

Amy was hinting at the fundamental difference between Green Briar and Heartland. The work at Heartland was all about understanding horses and their relationship to people. Those two things could never be separated. It wasn't simply a case of getting the right result, which was all Val Grant seemed to care about. But Ashley wasn't ready to hear that yet.

"Well, whatever," she persisted, waving Amy's objections aside. "Just ride him first this time. Please. I haven't ridden him since — since the show."

Amy detected a slight tremor in Ashley's voice, and she looked at her in surprise. Then a realization dawned on her. Despite all her apparent confidence, Ashley had lost her nerve. If she hadn't ridden Bright Magic since the show, the chances were she hadn't ridden at all. Amy hesitated, then took Bright Magic's reins.

"OK," she agreed. "I'll warm him up first."

Amy swung herself onto the warmblood's back and set off at an easy walk around the training ring. Bright Magic was fresh and fretful and immediately tossed his head and broke into a jog.

"It's OK, boy," Amy whispered. She guessed that he was expecting to be rushed into action. She soothed him and brought him back to a walk again, refusing to give him an excuse to get lathered up. She rode on a long rein, giving signals through her seat and legs. He was well schooled and soon began to respond. He relaxed and stretched his neck out to accept the bit.

"That's it," Amy encouraged. "Easy does it." Only

when she was sure that he felt confident and calm did she ask him to trot. She worked him around the ring, helping him to find his balance and rhythm with some circles and figure eights. As she'd thought, he didn't really have a problem. He was the perfect show horse, sensitive and obedient but with massive reserves of strength and power. Riding him reminded Amy of riding Storm. They sure would be a match for each other, if only Bright Magic were ridden the right way.

When she had cantered him around the ring a few times, Amy rode over to Ashley. "He's going fine now," she said. "I think we could try a couple of fences. Nothing too daunting, just two or three nice spreads. Could you set something up?"

Ashley called a groom to help her, and the fences were soon ready. Amy turned Bright Magic toward the first. Immediately, he tossed his head and plunged toward the jump. Amy let him go, and he made an enormous leap, almost unseating her.

"Hey, steady," said Amy, bringing him back to a trot. Bright Magic was obviously still expecting to be driven hard and fast over the jumps. She took him back down to the end of the ring and made him relax before trying again. This time, he didn't rush quite as much, and Amy felt she was getting somewhere.

She repeated the pattern, asking Bright Magic to relax, taking him over a fence, relaxing him again, until he was jumping freely and easily, judging the fences correctly, and popping over them without overjumping. Then she rode over to the fence and slipped off.

Ashley looked amazed. "How did you do that?" she asked. "He's going so well for you. Why won't he do the same for me?"

"I think he started to rush because he was tense," said Amy. "If a horse is feeling pressured and anxious, he may become nervous and lose confidence in his rider. Rushing is just a way of getting the jump over and done with. Somehow, your riding must have been making him anxious." She handed the reins to Ashley. "So we need to find out why."

Ashley stared at the reins in Amy's outstretched hand, then slowly reached and took them. She mounted, looking pale.

"Don't think about jumping today," said Amy. "Just work on getting him to relax. That probably means relaxing yourself."

"OK," said Ashley.

She rode off around the ring, with Amy watching her critically. Quickly, Amy saw what the trouble was. Ashley was a talented rider, but her riding style was completely unsuited to a horse like Bright Magic. Although he was well schooled, he was a free and natural mover, and the way Ashley rode hampered him. She didn't give him her trust — she wouldn't give his neck muscles any freedom, and she was always ready to chastise him with her crop. Already, as they set off around the ring, Amy could read the lines of tension along his body.

"Give me your crop," called Amy, "and ride him on a looser rein."

"But I need my crop!" protested Ashley. "He's too head-strong."

"No, he isn't," Amy reassured her, running alongside and taking the crop. "He just needs more freedom to relax."

Reluctantly, Ashley did as Amy suggested. Bright Magic, sensing Ashley's anxiety, didn't respond as quickly as he'd done with Amy. But, still, as Ashley gave him more freedom to move, he became calmer and gradually lowered his head, reaching out and enjoying the room she gave him to stretch.

After twenty minutes, the difference was remarkable. Magic had lost all his fretfulness, and Ashley brought him over to where Amy was standing. She dismounted and turned to Amy with a smile of genuine happiness.

"I can't believe how much better he's going," she said. "And after only one session."

"Well, he doesn't really have a problem," said Amy. "You just need to build your confidence again and try to avoid letting him feel your tension. He needs an open rein so he doesn't feel stifled. And you need to take it slowly. At your own pace and his pace." She looked Ashley in the eye and said what she really wanted to say. "Despite what your mother may think."

Chapter Eight

A flicker of fear and surprise came into Ashley's eyes at the mention of her mother, but she quickly masked it. She nodded enthusiastically. "I'll be able to work him a few days this week," she said. "Mom has a lot going on. Then I'll show her how he's going for me. I'm sure she'll appreciate the difference." She gave Amy a dazzling smile.

Amy grinned in spite of herself. She couldn't help but be pleased at how things had gone. She just hoped that Bright Magic would be given the chance he deserved.

"Let's take Magic up to the yard, then we can get something to drink," said Ashley.

"Oh, I'm not sure," said Amy. "I should be getting back to Heartland."

"Don't you have time for an iced tea?" pushed Ashley. "You must be thirsty. I know I am."

Amy had to admit that she was. They left the ring and walked up toward the main block of stables.

As they did so, Amy spotted a familiar figure pushing a wheelbarrow across the yard. "Daniel!" she called.

He turned abruptly, and Amy waved. Daniel's face broke into a wide smile, and he jogged over.

"Amy!" he exclaimed. "What are you doing here?"

Daniel looked astonished to see her. He knew she didn't like Green Briar and its training methods.

Amy opened her mouth to answer, but Ashley shot her a warning look. "Oh, I was kind of just passing by," she said casually.

"How's Storm going?" asked Daniel. "When's your next show?"

"He's fine," said Amy. "We're entered at Melton, next Saturday. Will you be coming?"

Daniel shrugged, looking slightly embarrassed.

"It's not up to Daniel to decide," said Ashley. "My mom chooses which stable hands come to the shows."

Amy gave Daniel a sympathetic look. So much had changed for him. Only a few weeks ago, he was choosing which shows to enter with his own horse.

Ashley caught Amy's look and frowned. "Daniel's really lucky, Amy," she said. "Mom likes him. He gets to ride a lot of horses here."

It's not the same, thought Amy. And from Daniel's expression she knew he was thinking the same thing. But she said nothing.

"I know that, Ashley," said Daniel in a polite voice. "They're just not Amber, that's all."

Ashley showed no signs of understanding. She handed him Bright Magic's reins. "Take him in and rub him down, will you?" she said.

"Sure," said Daniel, but Amy could see he was fighting his annoyance. So was she. Whatever Ashley's problems might be, she was so used to ordering everyone around and getting her own way that she couldn't see other people's feelings when they hit her in the face. She threw Daniel a knowing look, then turned and followed Ashley into the house.

Ashley quickly got two tumblers and a pitcher of iced tea. "Sweetened, with lemon?" she asked Amy.

Amy suppressed a grin. "It's fine just as it is, thanks," she said.

They sat down at the big breakfast bar that jutted into the kitchen, and Amy took a sip of her tea. Ashley drew hers toward her and gave Amy a confidential look. "So," she said, "now that we've dealt with the horses, we can talk about the really important matters. How's the big romance going?"

Amy spluttered slightly. "Excuse me?"

"Come on, Amy," said Ashley, opening her big blue eyes wide. "You and Ty. Why are you so shy about it?"

Amy was taken aback. She barely had time to think. "I'm not shy. It's just between me and Ty, that's all," she responded honestly.

Ashley scrutinized her closely. "So aren't you going to ask about me and Matt?"

Amy shrugged. "It's none of my business, Ashley," she said. Then she reflected that she wasn't being quite fair. After all, she had talked about Ashley happily enough with Matt only the day before. She hesitated. "Actually, I saw Matt yesterday," she confessed.

"Really?" exclaimed Ashley. She searched Amy's face. "How was he?"

"Fine," said Amy, now feeling embarrassed. The last thing she wanted was to be some kind of go-between for these two, but Ashley seemed determined to talk about it.

"Did he talk about me?" she asked.

Amy couldn't deny it. She nodded. "A little," she said vaguely.

Ashley stared at Amy, her face suddenly open and vulnerable. "Amy," she said, struggling to find the words, "I know you won't tell me what Matt said. You're way too loyal, I know that. But — the thing is — I know it was my fault that we broke up. I haven't been fair to him.

And it wasn't just once — it was a lot of times. I just can't seem to help it."

She paused, and Amy saw that she had tears in her eyes. Ashley went on. "I know you think I'm spoiled with everything I have here. But it doesn't make up for losing Matt." She buried her face in her hands, then took a deep breath. "I miss him so much," she finished. "Do you think there's any way that he'd come back to me?"

Amy didn't know what to say. She wasn't even sure if Ashley was being genuine or just dramatic. Amy knew better than to answer for someone else's feelings, especially Matt's, whatever he'd said to her. "I don't know, Ashley," she said. "I — can't say. But I do believe that there's always a new beginning possible for everyone. And there is one for you, with or without Matt. That's the way you have to look at it."

Ashley sighed and smoothed back her straight blond hair. "You're so full of wisdom, aren't you, Amy?" she said. But she said it almost to herself, resignedly, as though Amy weren't there.

Amy felt slightly shocked. There was something in Ashley's voice. She sounded tired and bitter and disillusioned with the world. Amy decided it was best not to answer. She drank the rest of her iced tea and slid off her stool. "I really should get going," she said.

"How are you getting back?" asked Ashley.

"I'm not sure. The bus, I guess."

"You can't do that. I'll get one of the grooms to drive you over," said Ashley, a familiar tone returning to her voice.

She and Amy headed out to the yard once more, and Ashley beckoned to a tall guy in his midtwenties. "David," she called, in total control again, "take Amy over to Heartland for me, will you?"

❧

The next morning, Amy got up especially early, just as dawn was breaking. Boxer's escape the day before had given her an idea. They hadn't ridden Boxer before. Amy and Ty had agreed that it was better just to lunge him while he had seemed so listless. But now Amy pulled on her jeans and a sweater and hurried to get his tack. It consisted of a simple browband bridle with no noseband and a Western-style saddle. Both were old but well loved and supple. She carried them to the back barn.

The cob was standing in his stall, dozing. As usual, his hay net was only half finished, and Amy noticed that his ribs were more visible than ever.

"Hello, boy," she whispered, undoing the new catch that Ty had fitted to the door. Quickly, she slipped on the bridle and saddled him up. "We're going for a little ride," she told him.

She led him out into the pink morning light and mounted. She hadn't done much Western-style riding, but she knew the principles and took both reins in one hand. The main difference was in the signals for turning. Horses were trained to neck rein, which meant they turned away from the pressure of the reins on one side of the neck. This allowed the rider to steer with one hand, leaving the other free to hold a rope or a lasso.

She made herself comfortable in the unfamiliar saddle, then nudged Boxer forward. He responded willingly enough, and they headed out along the track that led to the outer meadows. The sun had just come up, and dew still lay on the grass, glinting in the morning light. Amy rubbed the last traces of sleep from her eyes and smiled. She loved this time of day.

Boxer plodded rather than walked. Mindful of how little he'd been eating, Amy didn't push him. They proceeded gently down the track until, suddenly, Boxer stopped. His ears pricked forward, and he snorted several times. Amy nudged him gently and he moved forward again, but this time with much more purpose in his stride.

Amy guessed what had caught his attention. It was as she had hoped. Boxer could smell the cattle. They rounded a bend, and there they were, huddled together, steaming slightly as the first morning rays of sun warmed up their coats. She rode to the fence, and Boxer snorted at the cattle eagerly. They stared back, and Boxer stood still, awaiting Amy's instructions. His ears were pricked, and Amy could feel that he was trembling slightly.

She rode him carefully along the edge of the fence so that Boxer could see the whole herd. He craned his neck toward them, his stride jaunty. Then she turned him and rode past the cattle again before heading back to the yard. She could feel Boxer's disappointment on leaving the cattle, but her idea had worked. The morning ride had returned him to something familiar, something that could help him adjust to his loss.

By the time Amy had finished with Boxer, the yard was buzzing with morning activity. She helped Ben sweep the yard, then turned out most of the horses and started mucking out. As she took the wheelbarrow to the muck heap, Lou approached her from across the yard.

"I thought I'd let you know," said Lou. "Ruth Adams just called and said she wants to speak to you."

For some reason, Amy felt slightly nervous. "Really? Did she say why?"

"No. She just sounded quite formal," said Lou. "She asked if you could call back as soon as possible."

Amy nodded.

What could she want? Amy wondered as she emptied the barrow and made her way to the farmhouse. Amy took off her muddy boots and went to the phone. She punched in the number for Meadowbridge.

Ruth answered the phone almost at once.

"Hello, Ruth," said Amy. "This is Amy. I'm returning your call."

"Ah, yes, Amy," said Ruth. She sounded cold but calm. "Martha tells me you paid us a visit."

"That's right," said Amy, surprised to find that her heart was pounding as she realized that she hadn't warned Ruth that she'd be coming by. "I wanted to speak to your father."

"Would you mind telling me why?" asked Ruth.

It was obvious that Ruth wasn't very happy with the situation. Amy chose her words carefully. "I'm very concerned about Boxer," she said. "As you know, he hasn't been well at all since coming here. He misses Hank so much. I was hoping to find out something that might help the horse. Something to help him adjust. I wasn't meaning to pry, or . . ."

"Do you ever think about people, Amy?" snapped Ruth before she could finish. "Or can you only think in terms of helping your horse friends?"

Amy felt stunned. For a moment, she couldn't think what to say. Ruth's voice was so condescending. Ty's words flashed through her mind — *You really don't like Ruth much, do you?* — but she pushed them rapidly to one side. It wouldn't help to dwell on that now. "I — I'm not sure what you mean," she stuttered. "I'm really sorry if you feel I intruded."

"Well," said Ruth, "perhaps in the future you might like to bear in mind that there are some things that don't concern you. I sent Boxer to Heartland in good faith, understanding that he would be well cared for and sensibly rehomed. I did not expect an amateur investigation into my personal life — or that of my father. Do I make myself clear?"

Amy was silent, her ears ringing in shock. But then she felt her own anger rising. "But someone has to care about Boxer," she said, the words tumbling out. "Yes, he's a horse. But horses have needs, too. We make them dependent on us, and that gives us a responsibility. If a horse is suffering, it's my job to find out why, and in most cases that has something to do with people. Their situation involves the people who create bonds with them or misunderstand them in some way."

She paused for breath, but Ruth said nothing. Amy found herself continuing, pouring out the thoughts as they came to her. "And in any case, it's not just Boxer who's suffering. Boxer was everything to Hank, and you're keeping them apart. Maybe you think your father can't gain anything from his relationship with Boxer anymore, but I think he can. His memories may be muddled, but they're true enough. He still lives for the time when all he did was care for you and rely on Boxer to help him through every day. I spoke with him for ten minutes, but that much was clear to me."

Amy inhaled and realized that there had been a little click on the line. She stared at the receiver.

"Ruth?" she said with a quaver.

The line was dead. Slowly, Amy put the phone down. She felt shaky and reached for a chair. She was horrified at what she'd said. She had no right to say that sort of thing. Ruth was right. She was intruding in things she didn't understand, and she'd gotten everything out of perspective. She needed to apologize immediately. She reached for the phone again and pressed redial.

This time, the line was busy. Amy pressed redial again. Busy. Frustrated, Amy put the phone down and buried her head in her hands. She waited for a few moments, then tried again. She heard a recording: *This is Meadowbridge. Please leave a message, and we'll call you back. Thank you.*

Amy took a deep breath. "Ruth, this is Amy," she said. "I just want to say that I shouldn't have spoken to you the way I did. I was really out of line and realize I was focusing too much on Boxer and his needs. You were right. I'm really sorry."

She was putting the phone down again when Lou appeared in the doorway. "How did it go?" she asked cheerfully.

Then she saw Amy's face and stopped.

"Lou," said Amy brokenly, "I think I've done something terrible."

Chapter Nine

"What?" asked Lou, concerned.

Amy shook her head, unable to say any more. "I'll tell you later," she said, smiling wanly. She headed to the door.

"Amy —"

"It's OK, Lou. I think I just need a little space to think," said Amy, trying to look reassuring. She slipped outside. There was only one person she wanted to talk to at the moment, only one person who might really understand. And that was Ty.

Amy found Ty in the training ring, lunging Spring. She stood watching him, her mind churning. Ty was concentrating on what he was doing and didn't see her at first, then glanced over and smiled.

"Hi!" he called. "I won't be long."

"It's OK, finish the session," Amy called back.

While Ty turned Spring and set her trotting in the opposite direction, Amy ran the dreadful telephone conversation through her head again. Had she really been so wrong to go to Meadowbridge? She didn't think so. Maybe it would have been better if she'd spoken to Ruth first — yes, it almost certainly would have been. But even so, it hadn't been *wrong*. What was wrong, though, was what she'd said to Ruth. There was no getting around that. She argued with a client. That just wasn't done. She shuddered to think what Lou would have said if she'd heard her.

Ty brought Spring to a halt, then led her to the gate. As soon as he got close, his relaxed expression became one of concern. "What's up?" he asked softly.

"Ty, can we go and talk somewhere? Somewhere quiet?"

Ty looked surprised. "Sure. What happened?"

Amy didn't say any more until they were tucked away in the feed room, behind some of the sacks. There, she poured out what had happened on the phone. "I just can't help thinking of what you said, about me not liking Ruth," she confessed when she'd finished. "I think you're probably right, and my feelings must have gotten in the way. And that's so wrong. My feelings about the owners shouldn't have anything to do with our work here."

Ty took her hands and held them. Amy could tell he was thinking everything through and waited anxiously for his response. "Amy, don't be too hard on yourself." He sighed. "It sounds to me like Ruth is pretty unhappy. Think about it. Her father is disappearing before her eyes. And we don't know why, but she's living there with him by herself. That's fairly unusual for a woman her age. She probably doesn't have many people that she's really close to — and even if she did, she probably wouldn't have much time for them anymore, now that Hank's so sick. What's more, the farm is falling apart. Her whole past, her whole life is disintegrating fast. She's not likely to be thinking clearly with all that's going on."

Ty paused, and Amy marveled at his insight into the situation. She should have been thinking like this all along. She hadn't even begun to approach the situation from Ruth's perspective.

"Then there's the guilt," Ty continued. "It plays into everything. She probably is still confused about sending Boxer here. And about a lot of other things, too. She might feel guilty about getting rid of Boxer, and now she feels worse, with you calling and telling her Boxer is sick. She wants to take care of her father, like he did for her, but things are only getting worse. It's a whole cycle of negative feelings."

Amy gazed at Ty. "I didn't see it that way at all," she said quietly.

Ty gave a gentle smile. "It's easy for me to see it. I'm caught up in it, too," he said simply.

They sat in silence for a few moments. Then Ty began to speak again. "The point is this," he said. "Whatever you've said to Ruth — or done — isn't really that relevant. Her problems are much, much bigger than that. You just happened to get in her firing line. When you have all that going on in your head, anyone can become a target. You just fired back, and I don't really blame you for that."

"You don't?" asked Amy in a low voice.

"No," said Ty. "And I'll tell you why. I've never known you to dislike anyone without a good reason. You're very fair, Amy. You try to see the best in everyone. But unhappy people are some of the hardest people to like. And that's because they don't like themselves that much."

Amy nodded slowly and leaned her head on Ty's shoulder. "I guess you're right," she said. "Thanks, Ty. I feel better now that I understand things a little more."

They sat quietly for a while, both lost in thought. Then Amy straightened up. "Well," she said, "I've left Ruth an apology. There's not a lot more I can do unless she calls back. But we still have Boxer for now. I rode him down to see the cattle this morning, and it seemed to help. It'll be a slow process, but I think he'll adjust eventually."

"I turned him out earlier," said Ty. "He was looking a little more perky, and he'd eaten a little more of his hay net."

"Poor Boxer," said Amy sadly. She stood up and brushed bits of dust from her jeans. "If only his life weren't so complicated."

"If only," echoed Ty as they headed back out into the sun.

❧

For the next couple of days, Amy busied herself with all the work there was to be done at Heartland. She continued to get up early to take Boxer down to the cattle, but he couldn't be her only concern. Dylan needed a session every day, too, Major needed riding regularly, Spring needed lunging — the list went on. And of course, there was Storm. On Sunday she realized that there were only six days to go before the Melton show. She felt frazzled from the early mornings and thought she would love nothing better than to ride Storm up onto Clairdale Ridge and take him over the inviting logs that lay along the trail. But she was far too busy for that. If she was lucky, she'd manage to fit in a quick training session at the end of the day — that was about it.

"Are you OK?" asked Ty as she clanked a grooming bucket down irritably.

Amy hesitated. Ty had been so wonderful about Boxer and Ruth, and now that she had some idea of how much he was dealing with at home, it felt really selfish and stupid to complain about how little time she was able to spend with Storm.

"Oh, it's nothing," she said. "I'm just a little tired."

"Well, that's no surprise. You're getting up before the crack of dawn every day. You should take some time out. What are you working on now?"

"I was going to groom Major. He needs to be ridden, but he's covered in mud."

"Let me take care of him," said Ty. "I'm finished with everything else I need to do."

Amy looked at Ty uncertainly. "Are you sure?"

"Of course. Go, before I change my mind!" Ty assured her with a grin.

Amy's heart leaped. Clairdale Ridge beckoned after all.

℞

Storm was as glad to get out into the open as Amy, and Amy felt exhilarated as he cantered along the ridge in the summer sun. They reached the cluster of logs, and Storm flew over them joyfully. Amy laughed out loud as he gave a playful buck, and she turned him back to jump them again before continuing with the ride. There was so little time at Heartland, she reflected, to just enjoy riding a horse like Storm, a horse full of life and energy and talent. Too little time. But still, she had to make the most of what she had and remember how lucky she was. It wasn't a lot to ask.

Feeling contented and refreshed, Amy turned Storm onto the homeward stretch, and they were soon approaching Heartland. As Amy rode Storm into the yard, she noticed a car in the driveway. Amy frowned. Whose was it? Then she took a second look and stared. Her heart began to thump. She knew that car; it had been here before. It belonged to Ruth Adams.

Quickly, Amy dismounted, and, as she did so, Ruth got out of the car. Amy stood holding Storm's reins, uncertain how to respond.

"Hello, Ruth," she said awkwardly as Ruth approached.

"Amy," said Ruth. She held out her hand, and Amy shook it warily. If anything, Ruth seemed to be slightly nervous. She cleared her throat. "I wonder if I could talk to you," she said.

"Of course," said Amy quietly. "Let me just see to Storm."

"Whenever you're ready," said Ruth. "I'll wait in my car."

"Please, go ahead into the house," said Amy. "I won't be long."

"I'd prefer to wait here," Ruth said firmly.

"OK," said Amy, leading Storm to his stall. She took off his tack, fumbling with the buckles and wondering what was coming next. Whatever Ruth had to say, she wasn't looking forward to it.

❧

"Please come in," Amy said politely, opening the farmhouse door.

Ruth stepped into the kitchen.

"Would you like something to drink?" asked Amy. Ruth was standing tensely by the kitchen table. "Oh, please sit down."

Ruth shook her head and sat down. "No, thanks. This shouldn't take long."

"OK," said Amy, pulling out a chair for herself.

There was an awkward silence, and then both of them spoke at once.

"I hope you got my message," began Amy.

"I just wanted to say," started Ruth.

Both stopped and smiled nervously.

"I hope you can accept my apology," Amy managed to get out. "I really shouldn't have said those things."

"Yes — I — I wanted to apologize myself, actually," said Ruth. "That's why I came."

Amy swallowed and looked at Ruth in surprise. This wasn't what she'd been expecting. She waited for Ruth to continue.

"It was something you said," explained Ruth. "Something you said just before I put the phone down. I couldn't get it out of my mind. You said that even though my father's thoughts are getting muddled, his memories are true enough. That was it. *True enough.* I realized there was something very important in that."

Amy listened, wondering where this was going.

"And I haven't been fair," Ruth continued. "Everything's just been too much, and — I just couldn't see what was true. What in all this was real."

Her voice broke. She struggled to regain control of herself, but she didn't manage it. She pressed her fingers to her eyelids, and Amy saw two tears escaping at the edges. Then she took her hands away and looked directly at Amy, the tears still standing in her eyes.

"I imagine you don't know very much about Alzheimer's," she said. There was no accusation in her tone; she was simply stating a fact.

"Not much," Amy admitted. "But I'd like to understand more."

"Alzheimer's is barely noticeable at first," Ruth went on. "Just simple forgetfulness. Then, as it gets worse, the person begins to understand that there's something wrong with his mind. It's very frightening."

"It must be terrible," said Amy.

"It is," said Ruth. "What's worse is that, at that stage, it's often accompanied by all sorts of mood swings. People respond differently, I'm told, but my father's reaction was quite common. He's a proud man, and he denied that anything was happening. Things would be missing around the house, and he'd get furious about it. He'd blame me, accuse me of hiding things. He'd put on two shirts, one on top of the other, and fly into a rage if I tried to point it out. Things like that."

Amy thought of Hank's mild, gentle air and stared at Ruth in surprise. Ruth must have registered her expression. "I know what you're thinking," she said. "You can't believe that Hank would behave like that. Well, he did. It wasn't his fault, but it wasn't my fault, either, and I had to handle it pretty much" — her voice broke again — "on my own."

"There was no one to help you?" asked Amy.

A look of frustration and anger came into Ruth's eyes as more tears fell down her cheeks. "Can't you see?" she whispered fiercely. "Can't you *see*?"

Amy's throat felt dry. She felt she was missing something. She was forced to shake her head. "See what?" she asked.

Ruth dashed the tears from her eyes once more and began to talk about her past. "They were very different, my parents. My mother loved to read and learn, but my father just lived for the farm. I was an only child, and my mother doted on me. She encouraged me to be like her, and I never really liked farming.

"Then my mother died when I was seventeen. My father was determined to do right by me. The farm was struggling, but he wanted me to fulfill my dream of going to college and becoming a teacher. Later, I could see how much it was costing him, but he never complained. He got rid of all the other workers, and the horses we used to have for them. He and I lived on the farm on our own. He taught me to be proud. We might not be rich, but we could hold our heads high because we worked hard. We didn't have many visitors. It was just him and me. Time passed, and I never left home. I couldn't leave my father on his own, not after everything he'd done for me. So I never married, or . . ."

Ruth trailed off. Amy's heart filled with sadness. How strange and lonely people's lives could be. But she was beginning to understand.

"You didn't want to ask for help when your father got sick?" she asked tentatively.

"No. I was determined to manage on my own. I didn't want people seeing Daddy like that."

Amy nodded. "But you had to in the end."

"Yes," whispered Ruth. "Everything was falling apart. The cattle began to suffer, and I got someone to sell them off. That sent Daddy into such a rage." Ruth shuddered slightly. "Then there was just Boxer, and I didn't dare sell him. I found Martha, and things started to improve — in a way. Gradually, as my father deteriorated, he became less aggressive. He no longer had a grasp on what was happening to him. I thought he couldn't really care anymore, about anything . . . not Boxer. Not even me. That's when I thought that maybe, just maybe, it would be OK to let Boxer go."

Ruth's voice dropped at the end so that Amy could barely hear her. She buried her face in her hands once more and sobbed. Amy felt a lump rise in her throat, and she reached across the table to touch Ruth's arm.

"So I sent Boxer here," Ruth finished. She looked up again, her tearstained face full of anguish. "It was expensive, keeping him at home, and I didn't believe it could matter, after everything that's happened. Not for Hank . . . especially not for Boxer. He's just a horse."

Amy held on to Ruth's arm, her eyes full of sympathy. If only she'd known all this before. "Don't worry," she said. "Boxer is in good hands. He is grieving, but we're finding ways to help him."

Ruth calmed herself, and Amy got up to bring her a tissue. Ruth blew her nose vigorously. "I didn't really believe you when you said that Boxer was having problems," she said. "I've always thought of horses as being just like cattle — farm animals. I never took my father seriously when he talked about how he and Boxer could manage together. I just thought it was his little joke, his way of reassuring me that he was fine on his own. But recently, I've begun to wonder."

She gazed out the window for a moment, then turned back to Amy. "My father's fading. I'm losing him too quickly. For a while, it was a relief that he'd moved on to the next stage. But now it's beginning to sink in. It means his mind has almost gone. There's so little that really makes sense to him, but I need to hold on to every scrap. That's why it struck me — what you said about his memories of Boxer. You're right. They may not be complete, and they're often confused. But they're true. True enough to matter. And — they're all there is. They're all I have."

Chapter Ten

Amy and Ruth sat in silence for a few minutes. Amy was thinking hard and feeling terrible for all the negative thoughts she'd had about Ruth.

"I'm sorry," she said quietly. "I wish I'd understood before."

"It's not your fault," said Ruth. "How could you know? There are still things I don't understand myself. I don't understand my father's bond with Boxer. I don't see how it can be so strong. Boxer's just a horse, but I — I'm his *daughter*."

Suddenly, Amy had an idea. She stood up and smiled. "Let's go see him," she said.

Ruth looked surprised. "Who?" she asked.

"Boxer, of course," said Amy.

She took Ruth out to the stable yard and got a halter

from the tack room. Then she led the way to the turnout paddock. Ty was just coming up from the training ring. Amy waved and motioned him over. Ty looked astonished when he saw Ruth but tactfully said nothing. "We're going to take a look at Boxer," Amy told him.

"Shall I come?" he asked.

Amy could tell he was curious. "Why not?" She smiled.

Boxer was grazing away from the other horses. He was gradually eating more, day by day, and his condition was improving.

"Wait here," said Amy. "I'll get him."

She opened the paddock gate and approached Boxer slowly. He looked up as she approached, and he whickered. He was beginning to accept her as a friend and willingly allowed her to slip the halter over his head. She led him over to where Ruth stood.

"Here he is," said Amy.

Ruth looked at the horse uncertainly and stretched out her hand to stroke his nose.

"Here," said Ty, pulling a mint from his pocket. "Give him this."

Ruth fed Boxer the mint. He chewed it slowly, then eagerly reached to sniff at Ruth for more. He whickered softly and nudged at her fingers, and Amy looked at his bright, soft eyes and pricked ears.

"Ruth," she said, "he knows you. He knows your smell. To him, you smell the same as Hank."

Ruth seemed slightly bewildered, but there was no doubt that she was touched. "Really?" she stammered. "How — how can you be sure?"

"Because he's not like this with just anyone," said Amy. "He's only beginning to respond to me because I ride him down around the farm every morning. But he's responding to you right away. To him, you're special."

Ruth gazed at the horse in wonder and reached up to scratch his neck. As she did so, Amy saw that her hand was trembling. Boxer whickered again and rubbed her arm with his soft muzzle. Ruth's eyes filled with tears. "I — I never knew," she whispered. "That they — they recognize people like that."

"Horses are very sensitive," said Ty gently. "They feel loss and pain and attachment. It may be in a different way than it is with us, and they can't express it like we do, but you can learn to understand what they're saying."

Ruth nodded slowly.

"I think I'm starting to understand," she whispered. She turned to Amy. "You've shown me something very precious," she said. "And I can see why you want Hank to visit Boxer. I think you might be right. It would be a good thing to do. For both of us."

Amy smiled. "I'd be really happy if you did," she said. "If you're sure."

Ruth smiled back. "I'm sure," she replied.

❧

"So what made the difference?" asked Ty when Ruth had gone. He and Amy were wandering down to the turnout paddock in the evening light to bring the horses in.

Amy explained what Ruth had told her. "You were right," she finished. "Ruth is having to adjust to so much, and it's a terribly painful process. It's strange. What I said helped, even though I shouldn't have said it. It was all part of her coming to terms with where Hank is, what he has left."

"And I think you were right to go to the farm," said Ty, taking her hand. "That was part of the process, too. When people are lost in their own suffering, it's sometimes good if other people take action. You helped her, even though she wasn't willing at first."

They reached the paddock and spent a few minutes taking in the silhouettes of the horses against the sunset. Boxer was resting, but he was starting to look more like himself again. Ty leaned on the gate, watching him.

"Amy, there's something else," he said in a low voice.

"What?" asked Amy softly.

"With all that's happened with Ruth and Hank, I've realized that dealing with my mom's problems can be hard, but I do what I can at home and then forget about it," Ty said. "It always seemed like the best way to protect my mother — and everyone else. But I don't think that's fair to her. I want her to know all about my life — and you."

Amy looked at the ground as she listened to Ty, trying to take it all in.

"I also think it would help me to have someone to talk to, someone who could understand. It's not easy to deal with on my own." Ty shifted his weight as he paused and looked around the field. Then his eyes came to Amy.

She looked up at him.

"Amy, I'd like you to meet my family. It would be good for them to get to know you. I think it would be good for me, too."

Amy smiled at Ty. "I'd like that," Amy said. She had learned so much about Ty in the last two weeks, and she was glad that he wanted to share more with her.

Ty leaned forward on the fence again and returned Amy's smile. "Thanks," he said.

Ruth phoned Amy and arranged to bring Hank over the following Sunday, the day after the show. For the next week, Amy concentrated as much as she could on getting Storm ready to compete. It was tiring, since she still rode Boxer out to the cattle field every day, but one morning she was delighted to find him waiting for her, his head over his stall door. He was beginning to find a purpose. And Storm was going well. Amy worked on his balance and nimbleness, to improve his speed around the course; if she wanted to win the blue ribbon this time, it was important that they shave seconds off their time in the jump-off.

On the Wednesday before the show, it occurred to Amy that she hadn't heard from Ashley since their session. It seemed odd. Amy wondered how things were going with Bright Magic and decided to phone Ashley. She called just before the Wednesday dinner meeting, and she was caught off guard when Val Grant answered.

"Could I speak to Ashley, please?" Amy asked her.

"Who is calling, please?" Val Grant inquired.

"Please tell her it is Amy," she replied after a pause.

"Is that Amy Fleming?" snapped Val.

"That's right," said Amy.

"Why are you calling my daughter?" demanded Val.

"I — well, I just want to speak to her."

"Well, she's not here," said Val.

"Could you tell her I called?"

"I will," Val said and put the phone down.

"I just don't understand it," said Amy to Soraya. It was Saturday, and they were on their way to the show.

Ashley had never returned Amy's call. "I mean, she could have let me know how she was doing."

Soraya sighed, exasperated. "Amy, you're talking about Ashley Grant. Thoughtfulness is not her middle name. You know that."

"Yes," said Amy. "But when I talked to her, she seemed different. She was still harsh and self-centered, but she seemed to know it — and to want to change. She's not too bad, you know."

Soraya shook her head, laughing. "You sound like Matt," she said, and turned to Ben. "What are we going to do with her?" she asked. "She's incorrigible."

Ben shook his head and grinned. He was driving the trailer, and Soraya and Amy were with him in the front.

"Amy, you can't fix Ashley like you do horses. There are too many issues," Soraya stated.

"Well, I hope Bright Magic's going better," said Amy. And she meant it. She thought of Ashley's brittle life and felt sorry for her. For once, she wished her well.

They arrived at the show ground, and Amy and Ben brought Red and Storm out of the trailer. Then they all went to the registration tent to collect their numbers. Amy was riding early, so she quickly returned to the trailer to tack up Storm and start warming him up.

"Amy, there are only three more to go. Then you're on," called Soraya as Amy and Storm finished the small series of practice jumps.

"Thanks," said Amy. She grinned at her friend. "I have a feeling today's our day."

"I hope so," said Soraya fervently. "You deserve it!"

〜

Storm's stride seemed effortless as he entered the ring. Amy felt as though she was riding on air. They cleared jump after jump, turning smoothly and cleanly around the corners. Amy's hard work had paid off. She left the ring to a burst of applause. Once more, they were in the jump-off.

"That looked fantastic!" enthused Soraya, running to meet her. "If your second round is half as good, you're a sure thing."

"Yeah, well," said Amy, sliding down from Storm's back and patting his neck. "We'll have to see, won't we, boy? There are plenty of people still to go."

She took him back to the trailer, then went to join Ben and Soraya at ringside. As she approached, she could see Soraya beckoning to her wildly. She broke into a jog.

"What is it?" she asked, squeezing into the space next to her friend.

"Check it out," said Soraya with a grin. "Your new friend. Large as life."

There, entering the ring, was Ashley on Bright Magic. Amy stared. Competing again, already! What was Ashley thinking?

The bell went, and the pair set off. Amy watched them intensely. Ashley had clearly listened to what Amy had said, because Bright Magic was looking calm and relaxed. Ashley's hands were light on the reins, and the horse's movements were fluid and balanced. He approached each jump with his ears pricked and no longer rushed at them, forcing his last strides.

Amy was impressed. Her one session with him hadn't achieved this. Ashley must have continued on her own and worked on his confidence as well as hers. Amy knew that Ashley was talented, but what she was seeing now meant that she could learn quickly, too, and she was able to put new techniques into practice.

As they cleared the final fence, Amy joined in the applause.

"You did a good job, Amy," commented Ben, clapping with her. "Whatever you showed Ashley, it must have done the trick. They look completely different."

Amy smiled. "I'm really glad," she said. She couldn't help but feel pleased. "Bright Magic looks so much happier. I'm going to find Ashley and tell her how good they were."

Soraya looked at her as though she were crazy. "Amy," she cautioned, "you may think that Ashley is a reformed character, but if she had any sense of decency she would have called you during the week. Or come and found you here. Why don't you let her come to you?"

Amy hesitated. Soraya was sensible, and she was usually right about things like this. But she hadn't seen Ashley's fear or heard what she'd said about Matt. She had to give Ashley a chance. "Maybe she feels awkward," she said.

Soraya shrugged. "Well, good luck," she said.

∾

Amy found Ashley near the ring exit. She was standing next to Val Grant, and they were watching Daniel run up Bright Magic's stirrups and loosen his girth.

"Hi, Ashley," said Amy lightly as she approached.

"Oh, hi," said Ashley. She looked at Amy coolly, and Amy's smile faded.

"I just came to say I thought you rode a great round," said Amy a little stiffly.

Ashley smiled her bland, beautiful smile. "As good as yours, Amy?" she asked.

Amy stared at her. Where had Ashley's friendliness and uncertainty gone? She wasn't sure how to react. What was she trying to say? But she didn't have time to come up with a response, because Val Grant butted in.

"We know how to train winners at Green Briar," said Val, giving Amy a pitying look. "I know you placed well a few weeks ago, but that was just an off day for Magic. Let's see how you and your horse match up when Magic and Ashley are at their best." There was a lighthearted tone to her challenge, but Val's expression was reproachful.

Amy's mouth opened in disbelief.

"You'll see what Bright Magic is made of in the jump-off," continued Val. "That's where the difference will show."

Amy looked quickly at Ashley. Surely she wasn't going to stand by and let her mother be so rude? Especially after she had helped with her horse! But evidently, Ashley wasn't going to stick her neck out with her mother around. She ignored Amy's meaningful stare and looked down, tapping her custom-made riding boots with her crop.

Amy glared at her and at Val. She was aware of Daniel staring in disbelief, too. But there was no point in saying anything. She knew from long experience that Val was thick-skinned. She did the only thing that made any sense. She turned on her heel and walked back to Ben and Soraya.

"You're not going to believe this!" she said as soon as she saw Soraya.

Soraya took in her expression. "Somehow, I think I might," she said.

Chapter Eleven

"After everything I did and all the stuff she told me — she really seemed to understand what I was saying about Bright Magic, and she seemed sympathetic to the way we work. How could she just ignore it all like that?"

"Calm down, Amy," soothed Soraya. "She's not worth it." It was five minutes later, and Amy was still in a fury about Ashley's behavior. "Ben's riding his first round in about fifteen minutes, then you have your jump-off to think about. What's more important?"

Amy threw her hands in the air in frustration. "It's just so —"

"— typical," said Soraya firmly. "Forget it, Amy. No one can blame you for helping a horse with problems, but if its owner doesn't deserve the time of day, there's only so much you can do."

"I guess," sighed Amy. "OK, I'll go and get Storm ready. Good luck in your round, Ben. I'll need to be in the practice ring. I wish I could watch you."

"Don't worry, I've got Soraya to cheer me on," said Ben, giving Soraya a big smile. Soraya grinned back, blushing slightly, and Amy left them to head to the practice ring.

When she got there, her heart sank. Ashley was already circling Bright Magic, with Val shouting instructions. Amy watched curiously, in spite of herself. Ashley was still riding on a longer rein and giving Bright Magic his freedom, but with Val instructing her, she looked more tense. She was gripping her crop in her right hand, and as Amy watched her approach one of the practice jumps, she gave Magic a tap on the flank, behind her leg. The tap wasn't hard, and Bright Magic only flicked his ears back before taking off smoothly and landing on the other side.

"What's that you're carrying?" she heard Val bellow. "It's not a feather duster, Ashley. If you're going to use your crop, USE it. Don't confuse the animal by tickling it."

Amy shook her head and returned her attention to Storm. It would be interesting to see how Ashley held it together under pressure in the jump-off. But now she had her own round to think about.

❧

There were nine horses in the jump-off, and Amy was the third to go. The first rider had ridden clear but slowly, without taking any risks around the course. Amy was sure she could do better. There was a shortcut she could take in between the third and fourth jumps. She would need to turn very sharply, cutting in front of the parallel bars that were no longer part of the course, then jump the fourth jump, the gate, at an angle. She studied the route carefully as the second rider went around. No one else seemed to be going for the shortcut yet. If she did, of course, other people would follow — those who dared. But not many horses had the balance and agility of Storm.

The second rider collected four faults, then Amy was in the ring. Storm snatched at the reins, eager to get moving. They went past the starting point, and he was off. In his eagerness, he took off slightly too early for the first fence and clipped the top of it. Amy felt her heart sink with disappointment, but she glanced over her shoulder and breathed a sigh of relief. The pole was still there.

"Come on, boy," she muttered to Storm. "No more mistakes like that." She collected him for the second fence, and he remained steady. This time he sailed over, and Amy turned toward the third. She knew that Storm needed to land slightly to the right if he was going to make the sharp turn successfully afterward. She angled him carefully, then heard a gasp from the crowd as he turned on his haunches and darted through the shortcut. One, two, three strides, and he was over the gate. Amy couldn't suppress her grin. They'd done it! Now they had to concentrate and stay clear over the double, the wall, and the final fence — and as Amy heard clapping and cheering, she knew they'd set the pace. It would be hard to beat them now.

"Brilliant, Amy," cried Ben as he and Soraya ran toward her. "No one will beat that!"

Amy laughed in excitement. "Do you think so?" she asked. "It was that shortcut — I thought I'd risk it."

"I don't think many people will copy you," said Ben. "It's a really tight angle."

"They'll have to try, if they want to win," observed Soraya. "The time's unbeatable otherwise."

Amy slid down from Storm's back and stroked his soft muzzle. "You did us proud, Storm," she whispered, remembering Val's words. They still rankled a little. "Whatever happens, you're a star."

Then she remembered. "How did you do, Ben?"

He shook his head. "Three faults," he said. "It was my mistake. We approached the third fence at too tight an angle. I had to circle Red or we would have crashed through it."

"Oh, that's too bad," Amy commiserated.

"Well, there's always another show," said Ben. "And your perfect round made up for it, anyway."

❧

Because so many riders had been knocked out by faults in the first round, there were only two competitors between Storm and Bright Magic. Amy hurried back to the trailer with Storm and then back to the ringside with no time to spare. Ashley had just entered the ring and was circling Bright Magic before the start. Neither of the last two riders had beaten Amy's time. She was still in first place.

The bell rang, and Ashley urged Bright Magic forward. Amy watched them intently. She was suddenly aware that she wanted to win. Life at Heartland wasn't about winning, but there were times when she felt a longing for that life — for the thrill, the highs and lows of striving to be the best. And on top of this, Amy badly wanted to prove Val Grant wrong.

As in the first round, Bright Magic was going well. Amy wondered if Ashley would attempt the shortcut, and guessed that Val had insisted that she go for the win. Ashley's face was set and determined as she came to the third jump, and, with mixed emotions, Amy watched them fly over it. They landed, but Amy could see that they hadn't aimed far enough right. At such a wide angle, the turn was going to be difficult. Ashley pulled Bright Magic around as fast and as tightly as she could, and he lunged sideways. There was another fence in their path, and Bright Magic had to swerve sharply to avoid a collision. Once he was around it, the crowd let out a sigh of relief, and Bright Magic continued on to the fourth jump. He scrambled over, but the extra maneuvering had unbalanced him. He hesitated on the approach to the fifth, and Ashley acted instinctively. She used her crop.

It was as if someone had fired a gun. Magic plunged forward and raced toward the double. He jumped flat, and as he cantered away, a pole clattered behind him. Four faults. They were out of contention. Amy let out her breath slowly. There were only three more riders to go. She was fourth, at least.

No one else managed to carry out the turn as Amy had. The last two riders tried, but one clipped the third fence and the other just wasn't fast enough. Soraya hugged Amy in excitement, and they did a little dance together.

"You two are crazy." Ben laughed as they cavorted back toward the trailer.

"I don't care!" cried Amy as Soraya whirled her around. "We won a blue ribbon for Heartland!"

❧

Amy's success put everyone in a good mood on Sunday morning. As they sat around the breakfast table,

Ben described every move of Amy's jump-off in the finest detail. Amy grinned, delighted. Then she had a thought.

"What time is it in Australia?" she asked.

"Why?" asked Ty.

But Amy could see that Lou understood immediately. She wanted to phone their father and tell him about Storm's performance. There was a wistful look on Lou's face. Amy suddenly realized how good it was of Lou to be happy for her and that it wasn't easy. Phoning Tim would only emphasize that.

"Oh, it doesn't matter," she said hurriedly. "It was just a thought. Could you pass the coffee, please, Ben?"

Lou smiled at her, and Amy smiled back.

"When are Ruth and Hank coming over, Amy?" asked Ty as he drained his glass of orange juice.

"Later this morning," said Amy. "I'll be sure to be in the yard to meet them."

🙠

Amy heard Ruth's car from inside Sundance's stall, where she was changing the bandage on his tendon. She looked out over the half door and saw Ruth walking around to the passenger side of her car to help Hank out. Hurriedly, she finished up with Sundance and headed to the driveway.

As she approached, she could see that Hank was bewildered. "Sandy's lame again," he was saying to Ruth, looking uneasily around the stable yard. "Billy can't ride him if he's lame, I've told you that."

"Don't worry about Sandy," Ruth said to him soothingly, as though he were making perfect sense. "It's Boxer you've come to see."

She looked up and smiled at Amy. "Hi," she said. "Here we are."

"It's good to see you," said Amy warmly. "Hello, Hank. It's Amy."

Hank looked at Amy blankly, as though he'd never seen her before. "Boxer's not lame, is he?" he asked. "I don't know what I'll do if Boxer's lame. It's not easy, you know."

"No, Boxer's not lame," Amy assured him. "He'll be very happy to see you."

Slowly, they walked down to the back barn. Hank started talking about Sandy's lameness again, and Amy marveled at Ruth's patience. She didn't tell him that he was talking nonsense. Instead, she turned his comments around until they made sense.

"Sandy's one of the horses Daddy sold years ago, when we laid off the other workers," Ruth explained to Amy in a low voice. "He's lost track of what happened when."

Amy was moved. She could see how difficult it must be to read meaning into the things Hank said.

They reached the barn, and Amy led the way to Boxer's stall. "Boxer!" she called. "There's someone here to see you."

The cob's head appeared over his stall door. He caught sight of Hank and gave a joyful whicker. The old man's face creased into a beaming smile.

"There's my boy!" he exclaimed, reaching to scratch Boxer's neck. Boxer took in Hank's smell and snorted, nuzzling him. Amy looked quickly at Ruth. Ruth watched her father with a great sense of love and hope, then she looked at Amy, tears standing in her eyes.

Amy unbolted the door so that Hank could spend some time inside the stall with his old friend and companion. Automatically, the old man ran his hand down Boxer's legs, checking for minor injuries or inflammation. "Why did you tell me he was lame?" he asked, standing upright again and patting Boxer's neck. "He's not lame. His legs are nice and sound, aren't they, boy?"

"No, he's not lame," agreed Ruth. "You're right, Daddy."

Hank turned back to Boxer and started talking to him. "Told me you were lame, she did," he said, with a chuckle. "Nothing wrong with you though, is there? Now, let's have a look at your teeth."

As Hank chattered away, Amy had a thought. "Wait here a second," she said to Ruth. She ran to the tack room and got a grooming kit, then she placed it in the stall with

Hank. "Here you are, Hank," she said. "I think Boxer needs a groom, if you'd like to give him one."

Instinctively, Hank picked out a body brush and set to work on Boxer's coat, grooming him with firm, sweeping strokes. He looked happy and absorbed and had lost his bewildered expression.

"Amy, may I talk to you?" asked Ruth in a low voice.

"OK," said Amy. "I'll ask Ty to keep an eye on Hank, if you like."

⸲

"We need to figure out how this is going to work," said Ruth when she and Amy were sitting in the tack room. "I can see, now, what a difference it makes to my father to come here. And Boxer, as well. And you know, in a way it helps me, too."

Amy looked at her inquiringly, encouraging her to go on.

"I was always so grateful to Daddy for all the work he did to help me," Ruth continued. "But part of me felt terribly guilty. I always thought he must be so lonely, working all day on his own out on the farm. But now I'm beginning to understand that he was never alone. Boxer was more of a friend to him than I'd ever imagined possible."

Amy smiled. "Yes," she said. "Horses can be the most faithful companions you ever have."

Ruth smiled back. "Thank you," she said softly. "Thank

you for showing me that." She looked around the tack room, and her eyes rested on Boxer's Western saddle. She gave a big sigh. "But things aren't going to stay like this for much longer," she said sadly. "My father will get more and more confused, and then he'll need round-the-clock care. He often forgets to do basic things for himself, like wash or change his clothes. I don't know how much longer it will benefit him to come here. But until then . . ."

"We'll keep Boxer," said Amy, suddenly knowing it was the right thing to do, "so that Hank can visit for as long as you think is right." She smiled at Ruth. "Boxer loves Hank," she told her. "And seeing him every now and again will help ease the pain of losing him. And meanwhile, we are helping him to adjust. Time's a great healer, for horses as well as humans. Things will eventually get better for Boxer."

Ruth nodded silently, and a tear rolled down her cheek.

"And for you, too," added Amy gently.

They headed back to the barn and found Ty leading Hank up to the yard. Hank looked vague and exhausted.

"I think he's had enough," said Ty.

"I expect you are tired, aren't you, Daddy?" said Ruth, taking her father's arm. "Coming here was a big trip."

She guided him to the car and helped him in. Then she shook hands with Amy and Ty.

"See you soon," she said quietly. "And thank you."

❧

Amy and Ty went inside, to find Grandpa at the stove, making waffles. "Just in time!" he exclaimed when he saw them. "Call the others. We need to eat these while they're still hot."

Lou and Ben soon appeared, drawn by the offer of Grandpa's cooking. "I made them as a special treat," he explained, serving the waffles onto plates. "With Amy and Ben both winning at shows so much, I thought it was time we celebrated a few of your ribbons."

"I haven't won anything!" protested Ben.

"Oh, no, nothing," said Amy. "You were only Intermediate Champion a few weeks ago."

Everyone laughed and sat down and began pouring maple syrup over the waffles. Amy explained how things had gone with Ruth, Hank, and Boxer. "So we need to keep Boxer here for a while longer," she finished. "He's settling in, gradually. And if anyone else would like to take him down to the cattle field in the mornings, that would be great. It will be good for him to get used to different riders."

Lou looked thoughtful. "You know, I'd like to do that," she said. "He's a gentle ride, isn't he?"

"Couldn't be gentler," agreed Amy. Lou's suggestion was perfect. It would give her more time with the other horses, and Boxer was ideal for building a rider's confidence.

"Let's do alternate days," said Lou. "Then you'll get a chance to sleep in every other day."

"Yeah, until six A.M." Amy laughed. "Thanks a lot, Lou!"

When the waffles were finished, Amy and Ty stood up.

"Where are you two off to?" asked Grandpa.

Amy and Ty exchanged glances. "We're going to visit Ty's family," said Amy. "I'm going to meet his mom this afternoon."

"Really? That's great," said Grandpa, smiling warmly at them. His eyes twinkled. "You need to be careful, though, Ty," he added. "Amy might have your mother on horseback before you know it."

Ty laughed. "Anything's possible," he said. "For Amy, anyway."

Amy grinned at him. His praise meant a lot to her, but she knew that she couldn't do anything without the love and help of everyone at Heartland. Somehow, together, it always seemed possible to find new beginnings at Heartland — and new reasons to look forward to the future.

MORE SERIES YOU'LL FALL IN LOVE WITH

TWITCHES

Imagine finding out you have an identical twin. Cam and Alex just did. Think nothing can top that? Guess again. (They also just learned they're witches.)

The AMAZING DAYS of ABBY HAYES™

In a family of superstars it's hard to stand out. But Abby is about to surprise her friends, her family, and most of all, herself!

Jody is about to begin a dream vacation on the wide open sea, traveling to new places and helping her parents with their dolphin research. You can tag along with

Dolphin Diaries

Learn more at www.scholastic.com/books

Available Wherever Books Are Sold.

■ SCHOLASTIC

GIRLT3